Choose Your Own Minecraft Story

The Zombie Adventure 3:

Plunge into the Nether

John Diary

For all the young readers and imaginers. For the heroes of tomorrow. We need you!

And, as always, for Sarah.

Hey!

It's me, John Diary, the author. Before you get started, I wanted to tell you something very important.

This book is no normal book! In this book, you, not the author, get to decide what happens next. Start reading it like normal but at the end of each section you will get two or more choices of what you can do next. Choose what you want to do and then turn to that page.

DON'T just flip through the pages of the book, because that will ruin the surprise! And also it won't make any sense!

There are twenty-three different endings in this book and three "happy" endings that will lead you to the next book, The Zombie Adventure 4: Beginning of the End. Once you get to one ending, go back and start reading again. There are so many stories in this one book!

ALSO, this is a sequel to The Zombie Adventure 2: Journey to the Ender. Three endings in that book lead to the beginning of this one. If you haven't found those endings yet, go back and find them! But if you haven't read the book, that's okay too. Start here! You'll figure it out.

Happy reading,

John

You stand beside the old woman at the top of the stairs, looking down at the pool of lava beneath you. Actually, it's the square of strange stone blocks above the pool that interests you. Each one has an open socket in it, begging to be filled.

I'm working on it, you think. This is an end portal, or it will be once you fill those open sockets with the Eyes of Ender that they desire. And then you can leap through the portal and go to the End and then, maybe, finally, you'll be able to go home.

You look down at your zombie hands. It's hard to get used to being a zombie and it's not necessarily your favourite thing in the whole world. The worst part is the nagging desire to eat everybody that you see.

You look over at the old woman. She is staring out at the pool of magma thoughtfully. *Friend, not food,* you remind yourself.

"Isn't it beautiful?" she says, as you lick your lips.

You quickly wipe your mouth and straighten up. "Mhhm, yes," you say quickly. And then you think about it. "Wait, you can't see," you remind the old villager.

She turns to you with an unimpressed look. "Yes, I know that, but I mean the idea of it, the power of it. It's a portal that takes you to a different world!" She raises her hands into the air as she talks. "Isn't that beautiful?"

You bite your green lip. "Well, you know, I actually come from a totally different world that isn't like this one at all," you say. "Everything isn't so blocky like this, I mean it's *really* different. And I just fell asleep playing Minecraft one night and woke up here. So, portals between worlds are kind of boring for me…"

"Fine," she says, looking unimpressed. "You're kind of a party pooper Rotney, did you know?" A little smile tugs at the corner of her lips.

You still aren't used to people calling you by your zombie name, it feels weird.

"Hey!" you say indignantly, but you're not really bothered. The old villager, Madame Mole, doesn't mean you any harm. She's already helped you out a bunch and she's about to help you some more. She's doing all she can to get you home. She brought you here because she said that she had something for you that might help on your journey.

Madame Mole turns and stares out again over the portal. You tap your foot a bit and look around. The elder golem from earlier is still standing in the room, totally still like a statue. *That guy's weird,* you think.

If you remind Madame Mole about the help she offered, *turn to page 5*.

If you wait patiently, *turn to page 8*.

A gust of bravery and just a bit of trouble rushes through you and ripples your shirt.

"Yes he will!" you shout. "Wait, sorry. Yes I will!"

The crowd of pigmen gasps.

The chief begins to shake, full of rage. The skull on her head starts tilting dangerously to the side.

"Well then!" the chief yells. "What are you going to do about it?!"

You think about this. Your eyes go slightly cross-eyed. *What* are *you going to do about it?* you wonder.

"No matter what you say, the people still support me! Right?!" The chief raises her arms in the air and closes her eyes, preparing for the roar of support.

She's met, instead, with a roar of silence. The crowd is awkwardly quiet.

The chief opens one of her eyes and peeks out at the crowd, trying to figure out what's happening.

You have an idea. You raise your own arms in the air and shout, "Who supports me?!"

The roar that the chief was expecting rises up all around you. You have to cover your ears against the deafening scream-oinks of the pigmen around you. You feel some grabbing at your back and you twist your head around, alarmed. But there's nothing to be worried about, it's just a couple pigmen trying to lift you onto their shoulders. You let them and soon you're riding on top of the crowd as it storms up onto the chief's altar.

You see the wide eyes of the chief staring at you, frozen with fear. And then, all of a sudden, she turns and runs off the other side of the altar and towards the edge of the island, the skull flying off her head as she goes. She leaps as she gets to the edge and goes cannonballing of the edge. You can only hope that she lands on one of the ledges below.

But there's no time to think about it. The pigmen put you down on the altar and one of them grabs the skull and places it carefully on your head. Then they all start dancing around you, celebrating their new leader. You dance with them, with your awkward, stiff legs and arms. The good thing about being a zombie is that it's really easy to do the dance move *the robot*.

After dancing for a couple minutes, the pigmen start to scatter and descend down the platform, leaving you and Gordo all alone at the top. You don't realize right away and look up from your dance to notice you're all alone. The pigmen are all around the altar again, staring up at you.

Right, you think, *I'm the leader.* You straighten up and try to do your best to look "chiefly".

Another uncomfortable silence hangs in the air as hundreds of piggy eyes stare at you.

You clear your throat. "What?" you say.

"Lead us!" one of the pigmen yells from the crowd. "What should we do? Should we build something? Go to war? Who should be imprisoned? What should the people do to be better, oh great zombie?!"

You stare off into the middle distance and then look at Gordo for help. But he just shrugs and steps further away from you.

What should I say?

If you tell the pigmen to go to war with the blazes, *turn to page 101.*

If you tell the pigmen they need to lead themselves, *turn to page 114.*

"Soooo, that thing that you said would help me?" you ask.

The old lady cocks her eyebrow at you.

"Is that coming?…" you continue awkwardly, "or… is this it? Is your gift to me some nice quiet time? I guess that could be helpful. You know, we're thinking, reflecting…" You look at her out of the corner of your eye.

"No," Madame Mole says plainly. "This isn't it. They'll be here any second."

"Oh! Good," you say. "Great."

They? There's a person involved? Who could it be, you wonder. The two of you wait for a little while longer and nothing happens.

"You know, the thing is, I'm in a bit of a hurry," you say, filling the silence.

Madame Mole shakes her head. "Oh yes? To do what?"

"Um, get home? Not be a zombie?" you say.

"Well, you're free to go." She says, clearly not impressed.

You stare back at the lava for a second.

If you leave, *turn to page 11.*

If you wait some more, *turn to page 8.*

"—We're going to go find a portal!" you shout. "You see, the thing is, there's got to be some players out there that have already built one, which means that we don't have to do any of the hard work! We just find some players, use their portal and we're good. Right?"

Gordo gives you the weirdest look, it's like his eyes are going to explode out of his face and there's a snake wriggling around in his mouth, begging to get out. But, then again, that kid always looks weird… *That's just how he looks,* you decide.

Awkward silence hangs in the air for a second.

"Okay—" you say, unable to take it anymore.

But then suddenly Gordo blurts something out. "How're we going to do that?"

"Oh, well that's simple," you say. "We're just going to—"

Oh boy, how are we going to do that?, you think. It seemed so easy. But where exactly do you find a pre-built Nether portal?

"—Go that way," you finish your sentence, pointing off to the left.

Gordo follows your finger. You're pointing right into a huge sea. The kid swallows and looks back at you, shaking his head.

"Ahem," you clear your throat. "You have a great point Gordo," you say. "I meant *that* way."

Without moving your arm, you slowly pivot around on your feet with little steps, until you're pointing off into the middle of a thick forest.

Your companion looks a little worried, but then you bet he *always* looks a little worried, so you ignore it.

And off you go.

You walk a good long time, and while you keep *trying* to have conversations with Gordo, he only responds with a shake or nod of his head. Even when you ask him the question, "What do you do for fun?", he just shakes his head.

"You *don't* do anything for fun?"

He nods.

Now *you* shake your head. You feel sorry for the guy.

You keep walking and you see a lot of trees and some mountains, a couple mushrooms, a handful of pigs and even a big green jelly, but you see exactly zero Nether portals. This is going to be harder than you thought.

You can see the night sky starting to get lighter and look around until you find a little cave and dart inside just as the sun streaks up into the sky. You sit and wait out the day while Gordo sleeps in a corner of the dark cavern. You spend the whole day feeling sorry for yourself for not having found anything.

When the sun drops down beneath the horizon again, you wake up a sleepy Gordo.

"What are we going to do now?" he asks, rubbing sleep sand out of the corner of his eyes.

You swallow and think about it.

If you want to go look near lava flows, *turn to page 76*.

If you want to get to know Gordo better, *turn to page 13*.

You take a breath and try to remember that thing that your mom always said: "*Good things come to those who wait…*"

Hopefully, she's right.

You think of your own saying: "*Those who wait around in a stronghold forever, never get home and end up stuck in a game of Minecraft for the rest of their lives…*"

That one might not catch on, you think.

After a couple more minutes there is a noise from the hallway behind you. Madame Mole turns towards it before you even hear it. You turn too.

"Here it is," Madame Mole says. "This is what we've been waiting for. This is going to help you get home."

The noise from the hallway gets louder and now you can tell that it's footsteps.

Who is it? Who is going to walk through that door? Your imagination starts to run wild. Maybe it will be a player all decked out in diamond armour, with a diamond sword and a whole bunch of potions who will help you just smash through the Nether and kill everything in sight. Or maybe it will be an Ender Dragon that you can ride around places. Everything would be much faster if you could fly… Maybe it will be a band of helpful wolves!

The footsteps get closer and then someone appears at the door of the room. They peak cautiously around the doorframe, and then, after seeing Madame Mole, they step out into the room. You're looking at a young villager with the biggest nose you've *ever* seen. He blinks quickly with his round eyes and his heavy eyelashes. He peers around the room and then his gaze settles on you.

"AiiIIIIIIEEEEE!" he shrieks. It sounds like a whistling kettle. He's so high-pitched that you have to cover your ears. "ZombiIIIIEEEE!" he shouts and he tries to turn and run. However, he's so panicked that his feet move in two different directions at once and he falls flat on his face.

You shake your head and look over at Madame Mole.

The kid in the doorway reaches out with his arms and drags himself along the ground, facedown, slowly inching out of the doorway.

If I had a taste for villager, you think, *this guy would be lunch, for sure.*

"Gordo," Madame Mole says irritatedly. "Gordo, calm down."

"He's trying to escape," you whisper to her.

"Gordo, get back here," she shouts. Then she leans over to you. "Sorry about my grandson, he can be a bit… excitable sometimes."

Grandson? Gordo!?

The old lady starts to walk down the stairs. You reach out to help her but she waves your arms away. She tiptoes her way down the stairs without falling in the lava (You sigh with relief.) and then feels her way past the golem and into the hall where her grandson is slowly slithering away.

Both of them re-emerge a second later. Madame Mole yanks Gordo back with a tight grip on his ear.

"He's a very nice zombie," she is in the middle of saying. "Not a zombie at all actually, but a player caught in the body of a zombie. Very mysterious. He needs our help in getting back. Rotney, this is my grandson Gordo. Gordo, Rotney."

You wave at the kid cautiously.

"Hey, nice to meet you. So…" you say awkwardly. A thick silence fills the room.

You break it with a hopeful question: "When's that help arriving?"

Gordo and Madame Mole stare at you blankly. "He's here," says the old lady, gesturing at Gordo.

That's exactly what you didn't want to hear.

"Gordo is going to go with you to the Nether. That's where you need to go next, to get the blaze rods to combine with the ender pearls you already have. Then you'll have the eyes of ender you need to complete the portal to the End." Madame Mole took a deep breath. "Gordo can help you with all that."

Gordo nods.

"Thanks…" you say, confused. Trying not to hurt anyone's feelings, you ask carefully, "But why *Gordo* exactly?"

"Oh, of course," says Madame Mole. "Because he's been to the Nether before. He can guide you. Right?" She looks at her grandson.

He nods quickly, his head bobbing like a woodpecker.

"Really? Wow…" you say.

"He's going to really help you," she says seriously. "I can feel it, you need him."

You're not sure about this. Honestly, the kids seems pretty… wimpy. He'll probably just slow you down…

If you take Gordo with you, *turn to page 16.*

If you go alone, *turn to page 14.*

"This is fun and all," you say, "but I've really got to get going. I'd really like to be home for dinner—"

Madame Mole turns quickly. "Haven't you been here for days and days?"

"Uh well, days and nights are shorter here than they are there. Time works differently. It's hard to explain—" you mumble.

The old lady looks disappointed. "You really should wait—"

"Seriously," you say, tromping down the steps, "thank you so much for everything, you've been great. But I've really got to go. I super need to find a portal to the nether, and that's not exactly going to be easy…"

"No don't go—" she shouts.

But you duck out the door and down the hallway, shouting "Thank you!" over her protests.

It's only when you're climbing out of the passage that leads to the surface that you start to feel bad for leaving a blind lady all alone in a hole full of monsters.

But you're too embarrassed to go back down there. Just as you're about to reach the surface you nearly trip over a small villager with a large nose who's on his way down. He smacks into you, looks up at you, screams, and then tumbles all the way down into the stronghold below. *Thump, thump, thump, thump,* he goes.

You squint down the passage. *Well, he can help her back up here,* you think to yourself and head out into the gloomy night.

You desperately need to find a nether portal so you can get the blaze rods that you need to open the portal down there. And the only way to get those blaze rods is from blazes that only live in the nether. If you were a player, this would be easy, or at least… not so hard. All you'd have to do is mine into the ground deep enough until you found a whole bunch of obsidian, take it all back to the surface, make a square out of it, light it with some flint and steel and walk right through.

But as you look at your useless zombie hands, you realize that it might be a bit trickier this time. You can't mine a thing. You'll have to find another way.

Luckily, you have an idea.

If your idea is finding a portal some players have already built, *turn to page 63*.

If your idea is buying some obsidian from a local merchant, *turn to page 74*.

It's basically useless looking out there anyways. And it's pretty rude to be travelling around with this guy without knowing anything about him. Even if you look like a zombie on the outside, you're still a living human being on the inside, and the only human thing to do is get to know your new travelling companion.

"I don't know," you say, putting your head in your hands. "This seems like a bit of a dead end. We could search forever… Anyways, I was wondering about… you."

A gust of confusion blows across Gordo's face. He spins around in the cave to see if you are talking to someone else.

"No, you," you say. "Like… how old are you?"

The poor kid looks mighty uncomfortable. After his cheeks turn bright red, he shrugs and says, "I dunno, I only spawned a couple days ago. Like maybe ten or something."

"Oh yeah, there aren't really years in Mine— in this world…" You tap your fingers against your leg. "So why did you want to come on this quest with me?"

"I didn't," he responds flatly.

"Oh."

"My grandma made me. She said you really needed my help. Said I had no choice. It was for the good of the… world." He said this last word very quietly.

She said what? Your silent for a second as you try to make sense of this and then you clear your head and look back up at Gordo with a smile.

"So…"

If you ask Gordo about the time he went to the Nether, *turn to page 40.*

If you give up and look near some lava, *turn to page 76.*

"Heyyyy," you say to the old lady. "I really appreciate this. I know you don't want me to go alone. But this is going to be a dangerous mission, it's not the sort of thing that you should take a kid on." You think that that sounds perfectly nice and won't hurt any feelings.

Madame Mole squints. "I thought you said that back at home, in your world, *you* were just a kid…"

You open your mouth to say something. But then you close it.

She's got a point…

You sigh awkwardly. "You know, I think I'm just going to do this myself," you say. "I'm an introvert. I need my alone time."

Prancing down from the staircase, you grab the old lady's hand and give it a good shake. "Thanks for everything. You've already helped so much, I really can't take anymore of your help, honestly."

She doesn't look happy.

"And you," you say, extending your hand towards Gordo, "*So* nice to meet you."

He shrinks away from your hand and yelps a little bit.

You turn the handshake into a strange little wave and get out of there as fast as your lame little zombie legs can take you.

Madame Mole shouts something after you as you go, but you just shout back "Thank you! Thank you!" and keep going.

When you climb up to the surface, you let out a sigh of relief. *That guy was a mess!* You're better off without him. And… like you said, it would probably be dangerous.

Do villagers respawn?, you wonder to yourself. *Wait, do zombies respawn?* You shake your head: you don't want to think about it too much.

You've got to focus on the task at hand anyways. You have the ender pearls that you need, but to make them into eyes of ender you need blaze rods, six of them. And the only way to get the rods is from blazes, and blazes only live in the Nether. Which means, *you* need a Nether portal, pronto. But you can't mine the obsidian and build one yourself, not with *those* rotting hands. You're going to have to find another way.

You think for a second, staring up at the darkening sky.

And then you have an idea.

If your idea is finding a portal some players have already built, *turn to page 63.*

If your idea is buying some obsidian from a local merchant, *turn to page 74.*

You feel bad. Madame Mole wants to help you so bad... And anyways, if she thinks Gordo will be helpful to have by your side, maybe she's right...

You extend your green hand towards Gordo. "Nice to meet you," you say. "Thanks for coming with me." He grabs your hand with just his thumb and index finger and shakes it gently.

You say goodbye to Madame Mole. She says she'll be waiting for you in the village, whenever you get those blaze rods that you need. You thank her again, and with Gordo trotting behind you, you head out of the village and into the night.

The two of you walk a little ways while your mind spins. The only way to get those blaze rods you need is from blazes, and blazes only live in the Nether. And everyone knows that the only way to get to the Nether is through a portal.

As you think, you call to Gordo over your shoulder, "So where do you think we should go?"

You hear nothing. Not even footsteps.

Concerned, you spin around.

Gordo is standing a couple paces back, staring at you, dumbstruck.

"You okay buddy?" you ask. Then you realize he probably can't even understand you, you're just talking in zombie groans.

Then, he nods. "I'm fine," he squeaks.

"You speak zombie?" you ask with surprise.

He nods again, a little more confident. "My grandma taught me... though she didn't know it was zombie, she just thought she was talking to some villagers with a weird speech problem."

"Cool lady," you say.

"She's the best," Gordo says with a confidence that surprises you.

"Alright!" you say, remembering that you have to figure out how to get to the

Nether. "What should we do?"

Gordo says nothing, he just stares at his shoes timidly.

You roll your eyes, but instantly regret it: one of them now feels a bit loose, like it might fall out of your head. *Dang zombie eyes.*

Gordo isn't going to be any help, so it's lucky that you have an idea about how you're going to get a Nether portal.

"I'll tell you where we're going to go—" you say.

If your idea is finding a portal some players have already built, *turn to page 6*.

If your idea is buying some obsidian from a merchant to build the portal, *turn to page 95*.

"Ugh," you groan as you keep rushing forward. *When is this kid going to stop being scared?*

"Rotney! Rotney!" Gordo shouts, scurrying behind you. "You really can't go in there!"

"We're not going to get anything done if we keep thinking like *that!*" you shout back and charge ahead into the village.

The villagers are mostly all hidden inside their houses at this time of night, but there are a couple on the periphery that are watching you carefully as you approach the city. You choose one of them with a long yellow robe and approach.

"Hello," you start. "I—"

"ALERT! ALERT!" the villager starts shouting, running away from you. "ALERT! ALERT! ALERT!"

"Woah, what are you saying, what are you doing—" That's the moment that you realize. It's the whole zombie thing. You're always forgetting about it.

But it's already too late. Villagers are streaming out of their cottages with torches in one hand and wooden swords, shovels and hoes in the other. They're charging towards you.

"Hey, hey, hey, hey," you say. But, of course, it just comes out as *"Gurrrawwwwwwwyk!"*

You pedal back to the outside of town, but the villagers are moving a lot faster than you can. The anger in their eyes is clear as they get closer. A horde of villagers is coming at you from your left and your right.

You turn to run and see Gordo watching you from halfway across the field outside of town. "Help!" you shout.

He waves his arms half-heartedly and yells something that you can't hear. Obviously, it doesn't do anything to slow down the raging villagers. They're on you in a second.

Smack, smack, smack, smack, go the wooden tools against your skull. You can almost see your little red hearts disappearing as each blow lands.

"Gordo!" you shout, but he's too far away.

A little kid villager runs up to you and swings a stick at your shins. That's what puts it over the edge: *Swlip.* You blink out of existence.

THE END

To go back to the last choice and try again, *turn to page 95. Or flip to the beginning and choose a new story!*

You can't just ignore the guy…

"What?" you ask, turning around just a little reluctantly. "What's wrong?"

Gordo catches up to you, huffing and puffing hard. "Thanks for stopping—" He bends over to catch his breath.

"You realize that I'm a zombie and my knees hardly bend. I really shouldn't be able to outrun you…" you say with a little smile.

"I know, I know," he puffs. "Gym was always my worst subject in school… Anyways, anyways, you can't go in there."

"Why not?" you ask. "How else are we going to get the obsidian?"

He gives you a weird look, then says, "You realize that you're a zombie and that your skin is green. I really shouldn't have to explain this…" he smiles slightly.

Dang, you think. He just got you, good.

"Okay, okay," you say. "That's a good point. But I can probably handle myself."

"Not here," Gordo mumbles. "This is Forestville, they have the best security in the world. A while back they had an invasion of skeletons. And ever since then… Anyways, you should," he clears his throat, "let me go first. If that's okay?"

You lean back and smile. "Sure if you want to," you say, but secretly you think that you probably could have handled it.

He stumbles off towards the village as you watch. There are a couple villagers that are roaming around the outside of the town, which seems a little weird at this time of night. Once he gets close to one of them, a villager starts yelling.

"ALERT! ALERT ALERT!" he shouts, and the other villagers start moving immediately, running out of their houses and towards Gordo. The villager draws a wooden sword and approaches Gordo cautiously.

You can't hear it from where you are, but Gordo says something. The villager stops in his tracks. He puts up his arms to halt the swarm of villagers charging up behind him.

"FALSE ALARM!" he shouts, "JUST ANOTHER VILLAGER!"

The swarm of villagers lower their weapons and with a chorus of annoyed mutterings they all return to their homes.

You're watching with your jaw dropped. *Good thing I let him go first,* you think. *Otherwise, I'd be a zombie kebab right now…*

The villager on guard talks to Gordo and seems to point him in a certain direction and you lose sight of Gordo as he wanders into the town.

You don't like waiting, and cross your arms as you sit out there in the field. You get as close as you think is safe, but the memory of that angry mob, keeps you from straying too close to the town.

A couple minutes later you see Gordo emerge from the door of a little cottage on the outskirts of town. He squints out into the night, spots you and waves you over.

You approach the town, wait until the guards aren't watching and slip past the limits of the town and up onto the porch where Gordo is standing. He holds the door of the house open and you duck inside quickly.

You relax as the door closes behind you, but are immediately punished by a loud scream that fills the cottage and pierces your ears. You turn to the source of the scream and see a villager in a long blue robe standing on a chair with her mouth open and her hands above her head.

"Shhh!" you shout.

"Shhh!" Gordo mumbles. "I told you that my friend was a zombie."

The woman gets down from the chair, straightening her robes and pulling herself together. "I know," she says, "but that doesn't make him any more pleasant to look at…"

You roll your eyes. "Do you have any obsidian?" you ask her. "We want to buy twelve obsidian."

She stares at you with one eyebrow raised. "What's it saying?"

"He's asking about the obsidian," Gordo says timidly and then turns to you. "I already asked her."

"Yes, I've got the obsidian, it's right here." She opens a chest in the corner with a swift kick and folds her arms over her chest.

You look inside. There it is, shiny and black.

"Now how are you going to pay for it?" She purses her lips and her nose jiggles slightly.

"Um," you say, looking at Gordo for help.

He looks just as hopeless as you.

"I'm going to need thirty emeralds, or you guys need to get out of here, right now," she says sternly.

Gordo is staring at you. "We can find some, we'll come back," he says.

Maybe, you think, *but how are we going to get emeralds, that's almost as hard to find as obsidian… Maybe there's a better way?*

If you go out to find some emeralds with Gordo, *turn to page 26.*

If you make Gordo pay and take the obsidian now, *turn to page 33.*

"You know what?" you say. "That walk that you were talking about actually sounds pretty fun. Kind of nice. What do you say? Will you take me on one of your walks?"

"You're sure?" Gordo asks.

"Yeah, just take me wherever you usually go." You can tell by the flash in Gordo's eye that he's flattered. He thinks you're being so nice to him! And maybe you are... But there's a flash in your eyes too. And if Gordo was watching, maybe he'd guess that there was something else on your mind besides just bonding.

He leads you out of the cave and you trail along as you cut back towards his home village. When you're close and can see the lights on the horizon, Gordo takes a hard right and leads you out into some forests.

After a couple minutes, the trees give away to tall reeds and soft flowing sands.

"I like to come out here," he says. "But you know it's been awhile..."

"Mmhmm?" you say, but your eyes are scanning the horizon madly.

"...I haven't been back since that day... since I got lost."

"I can understand why..." you say. "Did you get lost around here?"

"Yeah," he says, thinking. "Actually, I think it was just over here."

He leads you up a hill which is crowned with a circle of twisted and tortured-looking trees.

"Mm, not here." Gordo puts his finger to his lips and leads you down the hill again. "Maybe it was over here?"

You follow him around for a bit until he suddenly stops.

"What's wrong," you ask, looking around with curiosity.

"Um, Rotney," he says. "I'm lost. I got lost while trying to show you where I got lost... I really am a mess."

"Hey, don't worry about it," you say. You turn all around in circles. You're surrounded by waves of sand, dotted with the occasional tree or wall of reeds. "Just trust your instincts. Where do you think you'd go next? What's your gut tell you?"

Gordo looks at you. He's a bit confused. Why are you asking him this? "I don't know," he stammers. "Maybe over there." He points to a big pit that you haven't wandered into yet.

You quiet your objections that that's definitely *not* where you guys came from and just follow his instincts.

You climb down the slope. It gets steeper and steeper and all your attention is caught up in making sure you don't fall and more importantly in making sure that Gordo doesn't tumble all the way to the bottom. There's a risk of *that* with every step.

You let out a sigh of relief as you reach the bottom of the pit, and finally you have a second to look around. You do and then you wrap the exhausted Gordo in a big hug.

"I knew you could do it!" you shout right into his ear.

"Wha-What?! What are you talking about Rotney?!"

You answer his question by pointing.

He follows your green, rotting finger out into the middle of the pit.

"Oh," he says.

There's a Nether portal sitting right there, patiently waiting for you in the centre of the massive pit. It's the same portal that Gordo stumbled into that day. All he had to do was get lost again to find it!

You rush over to the portal and bask in the purple glow. Gordo comes up behind you, obviously a bit scared.

"We found it… Here we go…" you say.

You look back at Gordo. He looks absolutely petrified.

"Ready?" you ask.

He shakes his head.

"Come on." You grab his hand and step into the portal.

Turn to page 35 to go through the portal.

You shrug, there's no other good way out of this. You're going to have to look for emeralds, even if there's no chance of finding them. Any other solution would be dishonest, and that's not who you are.

"We'll get some emeralds and we'll be back," you say half-heartedly and Gordo relays the information to the merchant, who just crosses her arms and pouts.

The two of you leave the cottage and once Gordo gives you the "all-clear", you slip out of town and into the plains that surround it. You walk for a little time in silence. You just stare at your feet and try to think of a way out of this.

How could I have been so stupid, you ask yourself. *Of course we'd need money in order to buy some obsidian. Where are we going to find emeralds? Neither of us are going to be any good at mining. We don't even have a pickaxe. This is a disaster!*

You look forward at Gordo, who seems to be walking with purpose, as if he still thinks that you guys can just *find* some emeralds if you keep walking. *Poor, innocent, little guy,* you think. *That's not how the world works.*

You decide it's time to stop this silliness.

"Gordo," you say. "Stop."

He turns around with worry in his eyes. "What? What? What's wrong?"

"Come on," you say. "Get real, we're not going to find any emeralds. They don't just grow on trees. I mean, not without a mod…"

"Mod?" he asks.

"Never mind that," you say. "All I'm saying is that we don't have any hope of finding emeralds out here, we have to figure something else out."

"Oh. Okay…" he says. "You're probably right. You know, I thought we could just go back home and grab the emeralds I have there, but you know what you're talking about. What was I thinking?! That would never work!" He sits down on a rock, and dumps his head into his hands.

"Wait… what?" you say, after a second.

"Just like you said," he sniffles, "we don't have a hope—"

"No, the emeralds at home thing, what was that?" you say urgently.

"Oh, I was going to get the emeralds I've been saving up at home, but that's a dumb idea—"

"No, that's a *great* idea!" you shout.

"I thought you said—" Gordo looks confused.

"Never mind what I said," you say. "Let's go!"

A smile returns to his face and together you rush off towards his home village. You arrive, weave your way to Gordo's house, waving at Madame Mole as you go past. Of course, she doesn't wave back. She can't see you. Gordo shoves the emeralds in his pockets and you guys head back to the merchant's town.

You almost get caught as you sneak back into the town, but Gordo clears his throat loudly at just the right time to distract the guard and let you slip into the merchant's house. Gordo gives her the emeralds while you stack the obsidian in your arms. On your way out, you grab some flint and steel that's resting on a shelf and he tosses a couple more emeralds at the merchant.

You tiptoe out of town and find a nearby field to build the portal. You start building it, but realize your clumsy hands aren't the best at this. Luckily Gordo is there. You direct him and he builds. Once it's up, you hand him the flint and steel too and tell him how to use it. He gets the hang of it after a couple strikes and a spark hits the obsidian, suddenly lighting up the portal. A strange wall of gelatinous purple light stretches across the doorway of the portal.

You stare at it and a smile cracks your green face. "We did it," you say.

You look over at Gordo. He looks absolutely petrified.

"Ready?" you ask.

He shakes his head.

"Come on." You grab his hand and step into the portal.

Turn to page 35 to go through the portal.

Disappointed, the two of you decide to march back to Gordo's village.

Madame Mole is in her garden as you slump back into town. You wonder, *who does gardening in the dark?*

After a second, you answer yourself: a blind woman.

As you approach, she stands up straight and looks in your direction.

"You two? Wow, you were so fast! Good work!" she says excitedly.

You shake your head and then realize that won't cut it. "Yeah it's us, but we're not back with good news— wait, how did you know?"

"Footsteps," she reminds you. "Never forget about footsteps. They're like fingerprints, everyone has their own. What happened? Do you have the blaze rods?"

"No, we gave up. There's no way the two of us are going to make it the Nether," you say. "But thanks for your help."

"Nonsense—" she starts.

"No, we're done," squeaks Gordo. "Come on Rotney."

The two of you head over to Gordo's hut, ignoring the old lady's pinched face. Gordo gets out a pumpkin pie and cuts you a slice. You dig in. It's good. Not as good as villager flesh, but it's good.

Maybe you can get used to this... *It's not so bad here.*

Morning comes and Gordo says you can have his bed during the day and he'll use it at night. You settle into your new bed and stare at the ceiling of your new home. And after a little time, you fall asleep.

THE END

To go back to the last choice and try again, *turn to page 40. Or flip to the beginning and choose a new story!*

"Well," you say, "maybe you should go tell him that."

She looks at you. "No, no," she says after a second. "That's just going to start a fight."

"So what? You're just going to let him keep saying things like that?" you ask. You glance quickly at Spark to see how she's reacting. She's not buying it yet... "I didn't know that blazes didn't stand up for themselves," you say. "Interesting..."

"What!" Spark says loudly. "No! We do!" She thinks. "I do!"

"Doesn't look like it," you say quietly. "If you really stood up for yourself, I'd think you 'd go talk to Ember. But that's fine..."

"Okay, okay!" she shouts. "I'm going!"

She shoots past you and towards the door back to the main room.

You grin and trot after her. *It's all working out.* This was your plan all along. Of course there's no way for you to fight all these blazes to get the rods you need, but maybe, just maybe, if they fight each other then you can go pick up all the rods at your leisure. All you needed to do was start a fight and it looks like you've got it.

You slip back into the first room just in time to see Spark shouting at Ember.

"—think you're better than me?! You think you fly the highest! Or glow the brightest?! Is that true?!" Spark is raging.

Ember spins slowly and then says, "Yeah," defiantly. "Why?"

"Well, because, obviously you're wrong!"

"Oh really?!" now Ember lights on fire too. "Well, then, who's better than me?!"

"Ummm," Spark thinks for a second, words sputtering at her lips. "Well, me, for example!"

"THAT'S EXACTLY WHAT I'M TIRED OF! It's always, *'I'm the best! I'm Spark! I'm so cool!'*" Ember says, taunting her.

"I don't sound like that!" she roars back, "and I definitely don't say that!"

"You don't have to," Ember sneers. "You make it clear enough with all your showing off!"

All the other blazes have entered the room now. They're watching from the edges of the room, bewildered and concerned.

"Showing off?! I'm not showing off! I just can't help it if I naturally glow really bright or fly the highest! It's just who I am!" Spark screams.

"AHHHHHH!" Ember yells, spinning wildly. "YOU'RE! THE! WORST!" Balls of flame shoot off of him as his frustration explodes out of his body.

One of the balls hits Spark, fizzling and knocking her slightly off balance.

"What was—" she's surprised and then surprise turns to rage. "YOU'LL PAY!"

Fireballs start shooting out of her chest as she swoops up higher into the air. They all solidly strike Ember.

He gasps and screams and then fires back.

You back up as a solid stream of fire extends between the two blazes. The occasional fireball misses the blaze it was meant for and you don't want to be wherever it lands.

The room erupts with fire. You can't even see Ember and Spark anymore. The stones are singed and then the smoke clears and… there are two blaze rods lying on the ground.

Yes, you think. *Two down, just four to go.* You turn to the other blazes. *Now how to make you guys blow up too—*

Your nefarious scheming stops abruptly when you see the way the other blazes are looking at you. They're all looking in your direction and they don't seem pleased.

"*You* did this," one of the blazes, you think it's Flash, says.

"No— what?" you say, trying to sound innocent.

"We were fine before you showed up," Flash crackles. "But now…"

The blazes all suddenly light on fire. You quickly do the math of the distance between the door and you and the angry blazes. *It doesn't look good…* But you make a dash for it anyways.

Fireballs stream across the room, hitting you in the back. Your math was right.

THE END

To go back to the last choice and try again, *turn to page 99. Or flip to the beginning and choose a new story!*

You squint at Gordo for a second and then at the merchant. You cross to the chest and start loading the obsidian into your arms.

"What are you doing?" Gordo whispers. "How are you going to pay?"

"Here's how," you say. "*You're* going to pay."

"What!?" Gordo hisses back. "I don't have—"

The merchant interrupts your conversation in zombieish, "So?! How are you going to pay?"

"Ummm," Gordo says, stammering.

You balance the obsidian over to one arm and point at Gordo with the other.

"You're paying?" the woman asks him expectantly.

"No, no—" he stammers.

You peer down into the chest and see something glinting from the bottom: flint and steel. You dip down and snag it and head right for the door. The merchant spots the flint and steel.

"That's going to be an extra two emeralds!" she shouts at you.

You nod your head back at Gordo and slip out the door, leaving him to deal with. As you sneak out of the village, you hear muffled shouts from the merchant's cottage.

He turned out to be really helpful, after all, you think.

Once you've gotten far enough out of the village you find a flat and empty spot and dump the obsidian down into a pile. *This will work.*

Building the portal is difficult. There's a reason that zombies never build anything in the game: zombie hands just aren't well designed for doing delicate tasks. But you do have something that the other zombies don't: a human's brain. It takes a little while to get used to it, but soon you're stacking blocks like a pro. You jump up and smack the last block into a place. Your feet land on the ground and make a worrying *sploosh* sound. Zombie feet also aren't designed for jumping…

You step back, admire your work and reach for the flint and steel that you shoved in your pants. The last stage of building the portal is lighting it with fire. You kneel down in front of the frame and try striking the flint and steel at the base of it. The steel just fumbles out of your fingers and lands on the ground. The second time you try, the flint goes flying, smacks the obsidian, bounces back and hits you in the face. Attempts three, four and five aren't much better…

"Dang zombie fingers!" you mumble, and then without thinking you call out, "Gordo get— oh." You look over your shoulder and remember that you're all on your own. There's nobody to hit the flint and steel for you.

But you don't give up. You keep smacking the steel against the flint until the sky begins to lighten. But you're determined to finish this before morning comes. You keep striking, and striking, and striking…

"That's him!" you hear from behind you.

You turn quickly. A small crowd of the villagers is standing at the edge of the opening. The merchant is at the front, pointing at you and Gordo is stuck in the middle of them, held firmly by the two big burly villagers beside him.

"Get him!" yells the merchant and the villagers charge forward with their various wooden tools. *Uh oh.*

"Gordo!" you yell. "Stop them! Tell them who I really am! Gordo!"

He looks at you, opens his mouth to speak and then just shrugs his shoulders, saying nothing.

"Gordo!" you say, and then you're overwhelmed by an angry horde of villagers.

THE END

To go back to the last choice and try again, *turn to page 20. Or flip to the beginning and choose a new story!*

It's the strangest feeling you've ever experienced.

The world turns purple, and starts fading away as you step into the portal. That's okay, a little like you're falling asleep, but the sensations in your body are the strangest of all: it feels like you're being dissolved. It's like your body is a spoonful of sugar in a cup of coffee. It feels like all the little blocks that make up your body are breaking apart and drifting away.

You might think that would be painful, but it isn't. A moment later, you're still you but broken into a thousand different pieces. It's like you can see from all of those places all at once. Like there are a thousand little you all existing beside each other, all staring at each other and out at the purple world around you.

Byoink!

And then all your bits smack together again and you're just one person again. You're just you. Well, the zombie version of you…

You blink your eyes as they get used to seeing again.

You're in a low cave, the ceiling is right above your head, almost touching it. You regain feeling in your hand and realize that you're still holding tight to Gordo. You can feel him trembling with fear. You want to tell him it will all be okay, but you're a little scared yourself. This is a strange new world, who knows what's around the corner.

The cavern you are in is built of netherrack, a dark brown stone spotted with red. It glints and sparkles at you in a disconcerting way. Every block looks like it has a little fire trapped inside, just burning its way out. The portal is behind you, squeezed into a little nook of the cavern. There's nothing beyond it except for stone. But ahead of you, the cavern opens up slowly. It looks like the cavern opens up at its far side. There seems to light bleeding through the open mouth of the cavern. *What's out there?*

You look back at Gordo. "You've been in the Nether before, right," you say, trying not to sound as scared as you are. "Where do we go now?"

He shakes his head. "I only came here by accident!" he exclaims. "I just stumbled into the portal. And anyways I've never been *here* here before. I don't know."

Right, you think to yourself. *Well, he's not going to help much.*

You take a couple deep breaths and focus. You need to find a fortress, that's the only reason why you're here. They are dotted across the Nether, and blazes only spawn inside fortresses.

With that in mind, you start marching towards the mouth of the cavern. There are a couple of cracks and gaps in the wall of the cavern on each side as you walk, but none of them seem large enough to let you get very far. You keep tracking towards the open mouth of the large cavern and the warm light shining through it. Each step you take fills you with more fear. You almost *don't* want to find out what's out there.

Gordo is following close behind you. You can't freak out now, not when he's watching you.

You continue walking and make it to the open mouth of the cave.

You stare down over an incredible sight. The cavern opens up high on the wall of a cliff that looks out over an absolutely *massive* sea of lava. It fills the entire floor of the huge pit that you've come upon. At first it's hard to understand just how big it is, until you see a couple tiny spots of black on an island in the lava sea. *Those are endermen,* you realize. They look like ants. This sea is huge!

There's a little landing just twenty or so blocks below you which seems to be an extension of another large cavern. Something's moving around down there: it looks like a zombie. If you climb carefully, you might be able to get down there, but if you slip… you prefer not to think about it.

There's also a thin bridge of netherrack that extends out in front of you. It's only one block wide and leads to a massive block of stone that seems to protrude surprisingly from the roof of the cavern. You shudder a little, thinking of crossing it.

If you go down to the zombie below you, *turn to page 38*.

If you walk across the thin bridge, *turn to page 90*.

"Let's go down there," you say to Gordo.

He sighs loudly. He must have been holding his breath for a while. "Oh, thank goodness!" he exclaims. "I thought you were going to make us go across that bridge…"

You laugh a little and start carefully jumping down from brick to brick along the cliff's wall. After a second, you realize that Gordo's not following you. You look up at him questioningly.

He's just staring down at you and the path you're taking. "This isn't much better, is it?" he says.

You laugh again. "It seems like nothing's very safe in the Nether."

"A terrible place," Gordo mumbles. "What kind of fools would come here?"

"Just the most foolish ones," you say with a smile.

And with that he starts hopping down after you. He's pretty uneasy on his feet and with the number of close calls that he has, you're absolutely astounded that he makes it down to the landing safe, and alive.

"Stay here, I'll ask for directions," you tell Gordo.

With a bit of relief, you walk along the solid stone floor and towards the zombie that's meandering around at the far end of it. You see that behind him a new cave opens up in the wall. Maybe you'll explore there next.

The zombie has his back to you, and so you call out to him. "Hello! Excuse me!" you say in your zombie groans and growls. They turn around and you're a little shocked. Your mouth hangs open.

It's *not* a zombie. Parts of its green skin are patched over with soft pink flesh. It has half a snout emerging from its face. It's a… zombie pigman. You've heard about these things.

The strange thing is that the zombie pigman looks just as shocked to see you as you do to see it. *What's it so surprised about?*, you wonder. *Do I have something in my teeth?*

"Hellllllooooink?" the zombie pigman says questioningly.

You blink a couple times. They are talking zombie, like you, but they have a strange accent that you haven't heard from any zombies on the surface.

"Hey, sorry, I was just a bit surprised," you say trying to explain your weirdness. "I was just wonder—"

"Wow, I can't believe this," the pigman interrupts you. "You're real, you're actually real and you're here…"

"Uuuhhhh," you say. "Yeah, I guess so?" *That's an awfully weird way to greet someone, but then again he does have half a snout sticking out of his face. What did I expect?*

"No one's going to *believe* this!" the pigman says, shaking his head with disbelief. "You have to come with me! Please! We have to shoink the others…."

"The others?" you wonder. "Shoink?"

"Come on, will you go with me? Please!" the pigman insists, jumping up and down.

If you go with the pigman, *turn to page 80.*

If you refuse to go, *turn to page 65.*

"Wait, didn't your grandma say that you'd… been to the Nether?" you ask sceptically.

That can't be right. Look at this guy, you think. *It's hard to believe he's even been outside before today.*

Gordo gets real worried-looking and stares down at his shoes intensely. "Yes," he mumbles.

"No!" you shout.

"Yes!" he says a little louder and almost looks you in the eye.

You stare at him closely. His cheeks and his giant nose are flushed red, but it really doesn't seem like he's lying. There's a fire in his eyes that's burning almost as bright as the Nether itself. He cares about this! *It's real.*

"Wow," you say after a second. "You really have… You know, Gordo, I'm sorry, I underestimated you. But you're really a brave adventurer. I didn't see that coming…"

Gordo flicks a tiny cube-shaped piece of lint off of his long robe.

An uneasy silence hangs in the air, until you can't control yourself any more.

"But, but, but, *why?!*" you ask. "Why would you go? Was their treasure, or, or, was it just for the experience? Maybe you wanted to test yourself?" This guy is a lot more complicated than you thought. It is hard to imagine him doing something like that for *any* of those reasons, but maybe everybody isn't quite what they seem…

"Itwasamistake," Gordo mumbles.

You don't understand him. "What?"

"Itwasamistake," he says a little louder.

"Pardon?!"

"It was a mistake!" he explodes. "I wandered into it by accident. I didn't mean to go! Okay?! It was just a mistake!" He is breathing heavily. "I was out for a walk, you see and I got lost, so I was worried. And when I'm worried I stare at my feet—"

"I've noticed," you say quietly, but he doesn't seem to hear you.

"—So I was going on a walk, I like going on walks sometimes, with my head hung low and I stepped up onto this block and the next second I felt this weird feeling like a fish hook pulling me from behind my belly button, everything turned a sickening purple and when I looked up, well, I was underground, the walls were made of a strange stone that I'd never seen before. They looked like solid lava…"

"You were in the Nether…" you say. "So you just turned around and jumped back through the portal?"

Gordo swallowed. "I wish," he said. "But, well, I didn't know that I'd come through a portal, I hadn't even seen the first one, so I turn around and see this weird purple square behind me and I, I, I—"

"Freak out?" you guess.

He nods. "I ran away as fast as I could and almost landed right in an ocean of lava. *Ocean!* There really are oceans of lava down there."

"How'd you get back then?" you ask.

"Well I met this weird spiralling thing that started throwing fireballs at my face! One almost hit me! So, I ran! I ran as fast as I can and I accidentally ran into a dead end. The only place to go was back through that weird purple thing, and I did, and I got back here."

You look at him. "Wow. So that's it? You accidentally went to the Nether and only managed to survive it by dumb luck and *that's* why you're here helping me?"

Gordo looks at you and you can see his heart fall.

"Sorry, I didn't mean it like that!" you say quickly, but it doesn't remove the pout from his face.

"No, I know, I'm only going to slow you down…" he says miserably. "I don't know why I'm even here."

"Hey, don't be so hard on yourself. We just don't really have a hope, you and I…"
You stare out of the cavern into the dark. "I don't even know if it's worth continuing to search…"

Your companion nods sadly.

If you go on one of Gordo's walks with him, *turn to page 23.*

If you give up and go back to the village, *turn to page 29.*

Not one to just give up, you make up your mind in that second, that you aren't going to just stand and wait for the fireballs. You're not ash yet, and that means that you can still run. You turn, thanking the mods for every second that you're still alive.

You place one foot and then the other, starting to run back towards the door.

Maybe they haven't noticed yet.

You hear a fizzling noise behind you and it just makes you run faster. Your feet hit the ground hard and push off.

Two more steps and you are through the door and somehow, not crispy, zombie bacon yet.

You race through the darker room, towards the door that leads to the bright cavern with its lava sea.

You don't look back, there's no time. Even the split-second that that would slow you down could be the difference between getting hit with a fireball and making it out of here alive.

You don't know how, it makes no sense, but you make it to the outside door of the fortress. Gripping the inside edge of the door hard, you swing yourself around the door and to the right. You feel a clicking noise as your shoulder jumps out of its socket.

Stupid zombie tendons, you think, *not good for anything.*

You don't really care about the shoulder though, you're only interested in running.

As you come flying around the corner, you almost smash right into Gordo. You stop yourself just in time to avoid knocking both of you off the platform and to a fiery death below.

"Run!" you yell.

"Wh-why!" Gordo yells back, while definitely not running.

"I found blazes!" you yell louder.

"Isn't that what we were looking for!?" Gordo yells back even louder.

You glance to your right and see the room you just exited is glowing bright. There are four blazes drifting through the chamber towards you. The one in the front is making a crackling noise that sounds a bit like words. For a second, you think it might be saying, "*Hey, where are you—*"

"Yeah, but we wanted to find them, we didn't want them to find us!" you shout back at Gordo, pushing him lightly. "Now go!"

If there's one thing that Gordo's good at, it's being scared of things. He turns and starts running. You follow, right on his tail.

The blazes come around the corner and are drifting after you, not touching the ground. They are fast and they start gaining on you, getting closer and closer, without even trying!

"Stop running—" one seems to say through crackles and sparks. You're definitely not going to follow that advice.

The only problem is that you can't run any faster, because Gordo is stuck in front of you on the narrow platform. Pushing past him might be a big mistake…

You feel the air behind you start to get warmer and decide there's no time to wait.

The ledge is two bricks wide and you step to the left and try to run past Gordo.

He doesn't see you coming and one of his flailing arms hits you in the side. It puts you off-balance just enough that your left foot misses the platform and you tip over, careening off the edge of it.

Your hands shoot out, trying to grab at anything to keep you from landing in the lava below.

You *do* grab something. Unfortunately, it's Gordo. You snag his arm with a couple of your fingers and pull hard to try to right yourself. However, all it does is send both of you flying off the edge.

The two of you drop quickly towards the lava while the blazes watch from the air.

You sink into the lava and when you've totally disappeared, one of the blazes watching nearby crackles and pops.

"Overworlders are weird…" it says.

THE END

To go back to the last choice and try again, *turn to page 55. Or flip to the beginning and choose a new story!*

I'm not Gordo, you think to yourself, *I'm brave. I shouldn't listen to him.*

"It's going to be fine," you say nonchalantly. And with bravery pulsing through your square veins, you back up, take a run at it, and jump.

It's only as you are taking the last step that you notice something is a bit off. It's your legs, they aren't pushing you forward as quickly as you were expecting.

Oh right, you think as the world rushes by in slow motion, *these are zombie legs. I've never made a jump like this as a zombie…*

But it's too late. There's no time to stop now. Your foot hits the edge of the ledge and you leap.

You're moving too slowly. You know it. You arc up through the air.

As you reach the top of the jump, you look down and realize you're less than half the way to the other side of the gap.

You start falling, plummeting down.

Uh oh.

"Rooooooootneeeeyyyy!" you hear Gordo yell in slow motion.

And then you dip underneath the ledge and start falling towards the hot, glowing orange lava beneath you.

Your last thought before you plunge into the burning sea is: *Maybe I should be a bit more like Gordo…*

SPLOOSH!

THE END

To go back to the last choice and try again, *turn to page 51. Or flip to the beginning and choose a new story!*

Running will attract attention. Then again, if you just stay right here, there's no way they *won't* notice. You're not sure why, but you decide that the best idea is to just stay exactly where you are.

Your eyes are squeezed shut, waiting for the worst.

But it doesn't come.

When you realize that a couple seconds have passed and you haven't become a cloud of ones and zeroes yet, you open one eye.

The blazes are still there. And worse, they're all drifting slowly towards you. They're in a circle around you and the circle is becoming smaller and smaller with every second.

This is what they like, you realize, *they want to torture their prey and play with it before burning it alive. Well, joke's on them, I'm already dead.*

They get closer and closer, until the one in front of you is almost touching your nose.

Just get it over with already, you think to yourself. *Throw that fireball!*

But they don't. They just hover where they are, all around you. The room is almost silent except for the vague crackling of the fire that surrounds the blazes.

"What are you doing!?" you mumble to yourself out of exasperation.

The blaze in front of you erupts into crackles and snaps and your eyes flicker closed again, bracing yourself for the fire that's sure to surround you in a second.

But the blaze just keeps crackling and snapping, and to your surprise you realize that you recognize a couple words in the sound.

"That's exactly what I wanted to ask you," the blaze says. "What are you doing?"

You open your eyes, surprise painted thick on your face. You can't help but stare at the blaze, trying to figure out if you're making things up or not.

"So?" the blaze seems to crackle and snap.

"Um— wha— what?" you stammer.

"You're acting quite strange, you ran in to a room full of strangers that you've never met and then shut your eyes and froze as if you were a statue…" the blaze says. "Quite strange…"

Another blaze behind you,pipes up with slightly more high-pitched bonfire noises. "I think it's a game," it says. "We're all supposed to freeze in place and the first person to move, loses."

"Nooo!" another blaze pops in before you can open your mouth. "You all are quite dumb. This is just customary behaviour in the overworld. This is how they greet each other, by closing their eyes and being as still as possible. The stiller you are, the more respect you show!"

"Shh! Shh!" the first blaze shouts. It floats a little lower so that it can stare right into your eyes. "So, what is it?"

You stammer, "I— I— None of those. I was just… scared. I thought you guys were going to roast me!"

A loud sound explodes from the blazes that sounds like a fully raging forest fire. Your eyes instinctively close again. It takes you a couple seconds to realize that it's… laughter.

"Why would we attack you!" one of the blazes manages to say through their flaring laughter.

"I don't know," you say. "I thought— I don't know."

"We're not violent," the blaze in front of you says. "We're quite pleased to get visitors. And anyways, you're from the overworld. You're a zombie. Very rare! Why would we destroy something as precious as that?"

"I—" You're not sure what to say. You just smile and laugh a bit.

The blazes don't join you.

The rods around the blaze in front of you start spinning a little faster around the creature and it asks you a question, quite seriously. "That raises the question, *what are you doing here?*"

The blazes wait patiently for an answer.

If you're honest and ask them for some blaze rods, *turn to page 112.*

If you tell them you're just here exploring, *turn to page 68.*

"You're right," you say finally.

Jumping is crazy. The whole quest would end right here if you made that mistake. And your life might end here too… It's just not worth it. You'd be crazy to risk it when there's another *much safer* option.

You turn around and shepherd Gordo back around the corner along the edge. He breathes much easier once you're back on the thicker part of the ledge. You slip past him and head towards the door.

Turn to page 55 to go through the door.

Suspicious of the dark opening in the rock, you continue along the outside of the mysterious rock and along the ledge.

The ledge keeps getting narrower and narrower until it is only a single block wide. You turn sideways, pressing your back against the hot stone wall and step sideways along the ledge.

From behind you, you hear a long sigh.

Gordo is standing at exactly the spot that the ledge goes from being two blocks wide to one. "Really?!" he grumbles under his breath, just loud enough that you can hear him. "You're loving this aren't you!" he shouts over at you.

"No! I didn't do this on purpose," you protest, but Gordo just shakes his head dismissively. "I swear!" you add.

Gordo turns sideways with a '*harrumph*' and follows after you.

You keep following the ledge and soon come to the corner of the stone cube. Taking a deep breath, you skirt around the edge. With a sigh you settle against the wall on the other corner and continue along.

Before long, the ledge comes to an end. With your eyes on your feet, you didn't see it coming. The ledge doesn't stop entirely, it continues on the other side of a small gap, just a couple blocks wide.

You look at it carefully.

While you're considering, Gordo comes around the corner and sees you and the gap you're staring at.

"You've *got* to be kidding me," he shouts. "Don't do it! Don't jump! That's just crazy! We've got to go back."

You look at the gap again. You think you could make it. You've definitely made a jump like that in Minecraft before… it's possible. It's just a bit scarier, you know, when you're really *here*.

Gordo's protests scrape at your ears as you try to make up your mind.

If you jump across the gap, *turn to page 46*.

If you turn back and go through the door, *turn to page 50*.

"Calm down, calm down guys," you say. "I didn't know! Stop freaking out!"

For a second, the blazes are all silent.

"Don' tbe so hard on a zombie just because he didn't know something. Haven't you ever heard of forgiving someone?" you say, crossing your arms across your chest.

"You didn't know!?" the blaze asks in a high-pitched whine, like steam escaping a kettle.

"Yeah, I didn't know."

They're silent again.

You say, "I'll take your silence as an apology… But really, you guys should apologize."

"WE SHOULD APOLOGIZE?!" the blaze returns to a full roar. "YOU SHOULD APOLOGIZE! MAYBE, THEN, WE'D FORGIVE YOU."

"Okay," you say. "I can see that we're not going to get along. I'm just going to go." You turn to leave, but the blazes are tight around you.

"You're not going anywhere," the blaze says from behind you. And then suddenly your back erupts in hot pain. A fireball strikes you right in the back. You stagger a little, but you stay standing. Your shirt lights on fire.

"Hey, what the—" you say. "What's wrong with you?!"

"Oh, what's wrong?" the blaze says. "Do you not like being hit by a fireball?"

"No! Of course I don't like being hit by a fireball. What's *wrong* with you?" you snap.

"Oh, really? Well, it's fine, because you know, I didn't know…" the blaze says with an aggressive crackle.

"You didn't know that people don't like getting lit on fire?" You try to slap at your back to put the fire out, but your zombie arms don't bend very well.

The blaze lights on fire and shoots another fireball right at your chest.

Now *all* of you is on fire.

"WHAT ARE YOU DOING!" you shout, waving your arms around like crazy.

"I was trying to put the fire out," the blaze says innocently.

"FIRE DOESN'T PUT FIRE OUT!" you scream.

"Oh. I didn't know," the blaze says with what looks like a smile.

You feel the flames biting at your skin and you start to feel the world fade away, turning black around the edges.

"Sorry buddy," the blaze says, as you spin your arms wildly. "I didn't know."

The word starts to fade down to a single point in your vision.

"Hey, take it easy," the blaze says.

With a pop, the world fades to darkness.

"I didn't know..."

THE END

To go back to the last choice and try again, *turn to page 112. Or flip to the beginning and choose a new story!*

You slip through the opening in the rock and your eyes take a second to adjust to the lower light, far away from the lava that lit up the large cavern.

As your eyes adjust, you see that you're in a fairly square room. The walls are made, not of netherrack, but of bricks.

This is it.

There's one door at the far end of the room that goes further into the fortress. With no other choice, you approach it. The next room seems to be lighter than this one, there is a low light shining from the open doorway.

There must be some lava in the next room, you think. In the overworld, you'd think it was a torch or maybe a furnace, but you're starting to get used to this strange land you find yourself in. Here, light only comes from lava, random fires, or the low glow of the rocks themselves.

You march right into the next room and immediately stop in your tracks.

There's one other thing that makes light in the Nether: blazes.

And you find yourself immediately surrounded by them. Six or seven of them are filling the room. The closest one is just two blocks away from you.

You clamp your eyelids shut and wait for the storm of fireballs that are sure to come any second.

If you run out of the room, *turn to page 43*.

If you stay put, *turn to page 47*.

"I'm sorry! I'm so sorry! I really, I should have been more careful! I realize now that it was very rude. And I really didn't know that that was the only way you could get blaze rods. I didn't mean to insult you," you gasp, bowing your head. "Please don't hurt me! But I'd understand if you did. I was *very* rude. I understand if you want to set me on fire, but I beg you to reconsider. Please."

The blazes spin idly around you, just watching.

"I'm so sorry," you say again. "I can't believe what I've done. Roast me! Roast me!" You collapse to your knees, shaking your hands in the air. "Is there anything that I can do to make this better?" you plead.

"Stand up," one of the blazes rattles and cracks.

Well, that's easy, you think to yourself sarcastically, but you stand up solemnly. "Yes?"

The blazes spin and watch you.

"I'm really sorry," you say.

The blaze in front of you nods and then says, "Perhaps you can help us in order to show that you really meant no harm. If you went out of your way for our benefit, we would forgive you."

"Okay," you nod. "I'll do it." Silence hangs in the air.

"What… am I doing?" you say after a second.

The blaze shrugs and says, "I don't know, I thought you were the one who was supposed to be doing the helping." The other blazes around you start to loosen their tight circle and begin to drift away to different corners of the cavern.

You watch them go for a second and glance towards the door. You think, *I guess if I asked them what bothered them, I could try to fix whatever it was that got on their nerves… or…* Your eyes flicker back to the open door.

If you leave the room, *turn to page 104.*

If you ask a blaze about what bothers them, *turn to page 97.*

"You're right," you say in the best mysterious-god-from-another-world voice that you can manage.

Gordo pokes you in the back from behind. "Wha—"

You step on his foot. Hard. He closes his mouth in a hurry.

"I am a zombie, from the Overworld. I have been sent here to… check on you and I may lead you… if you treat me right!" You cross your arms in a way that hopefully makes you seem intimidating.

One of the pigmen faints. *I guess I was successful,* you think.

Two of the pigmen tend to their fallen friend while the other bows low again. "You must come see our leader! The chief! You must see the rest of our people!"

"Ah, yes, of course," you say. "Lead me on."

The fainted pigman is poked and prodded back to life and the four pigmen lead the way solemnly through a maze of netherrack tunnels.

As you walk, Gordo gives you a look which clearly says, 'What in the world are you doing?!'

You just shrug your shoulders. You mouth the words, 'Play along', and Gordo nods reluctantly.

Sooner than you expect, the zombie pigmen stop. You squint past them in the low-light. You've entered another massive cavern, like the one that was filled with lava earlier. This one's different though. The floor is far below but not covered in liquid fire and the room is dominated by a massive hunk of floating gravel that nearly fills the whole cavern. You look closer and see little people walking around on the floating gravel island.

The pigmen lead you towards a little bridge that crosses the gap between the ledge on the outside of the cavern and the island in the middle. A couple pigmen seem to be guarding the entrance. One of your pigmen companions whispers to them and they step back to let you pass. You notice that the guards watch you very closely as you walk past. It's uncomfortable.

The bridge is only one block wide and made of what looks like cobblestone. You take a couple careful steps. You're worried about Gordo and his infamously terrible balance. There's no railings on the side to catch him if he falls and the fall is so long that you can't see the bottom.

What's with this place and terribly dangerous bridges, you wonder.

Against all odds, you and Gordo make it across safely and the pigmen lead you to the far end of the island. As you walk past the fires, mushrooms and little buildings made of gravel and sand that dominate the island, the pigmen that seem to live there start gathering around you. There's more than you thought at first: a couple hundred at least!

Suddenly your guards stop and you almost walk into the back of one of them. Everyone's staring forward and you look to see what has their attention.

One zombie pigman stands at the top of an altar made of gravel. They are wearing a darkened, almost black, skeleton skull on top of their own head, giving them a creepy aura. They look at you and it seems like two pairs of eyes are staring right into you. Through you, even.

One of your escorts skitters up to the platform and whispers in this mysterious pigman's ear.

The skull-wearing pigman nods and straightens up. "Zombie, will you come closer so I may look upon you?"

"Um," you say. It's a weird request. "Cool, I guess."

You step forward and do a joking little pirouette. No one laughs. In fact, everything is silent.

"You are the zombie?" The skull-wearer breaks the silence.

"Yes, that's me. And you're a pigman," you say extending your hand.

"Pigwoman," the skull-wearer says with a twitch of their one non-rotted eye. "And chief of the pigmen!"

The pigmen all oink together making a terrible, overwhelming noise. You hold your ears.

"It is true then," says the chief. "You are the zombie, the creator!"

"Um, yes," you say, but you're unsure what she means. "The creator?"

She shouts, "It is said that the race of zombie pigmen were started by one zombie long ago! A zombie bit a pig and our line was started. That zombie, it is also said, will return someday in order to bless us!"

"Right," you say. "That is I! The creator!"

The crowd comes to a hush.

"Can you prove it?" the chief asks.

There are a rumblings of anger and confusion from the crowd.

"No, I—" you stammer. "I don't need to prove it!"

A couple pigmen cheer. One pigman in the crowd heckles the chief. "You must step down so that the zombie can become chief!"

"Not until we have proof—" the chief starts, but someone else yells from the crowd, cutting her off.

"Step down! Now!"

You feel a little uncomfortable. You didn't want to make someone lose their job…

"Does the zombie want it?!" the chief screams. "Will he challenge me?!"

Oh boy. Everyone's staring at you, waiting for you to say something.

If you challenge the chief, *turn to page 3*.

If you let her stay chief, *turn to page 82*.

"This way!" you say, shooing Gordo back along the ledge and towards the bridge. "Come with me and *don't* open your eyes."

You have a feeling that they wouldn't be too happy if they saw the brightly glowing lava sea beneath you.

You have to wait for Gordo to cross the narrow bridge. Slowly, you follow after him.

"What's taking so long…" one of the blazes moans. "I want to look…"

"Nope!" you say quickly. "We are waiting for something quite bright to pass. You won't like it at all."

The blaze makes a face as if you said something gross, like 'zombies are green because they're actually giant boogers with legs'. But it doesn't open its eyes. And that's all you care about.

Finally, you're across the bridge and you shepherd the blazes into the cavern that you first came through when you arrived.

You look behind you and they're all floating around inside the flowing cave of netherrack.

You open your mouth to speak to them and—

If you tell them to open their eyes, *turn to page 61*.

If you lead them through the portal, *turn to page 119*.

"Open! Those! Eyes!" you shout, and the blazes do.

They blink, turning around and examining the netherrack cavern that they're in.

"So… what do you think?" you say, with a proud smile on your face.

They don't seem so happy. But they don't day anything quite yet. One of them drifts over to the wall and scowls at it.

Weird, you think.

"WHAT!" the blaze by the wall screams. "IS! THIS!" It scoots away from the netherrack wall in a hurry, as if it were dangerous.

"A— a rock?" you volunteer.

"IT'S GLOWING!" the blaze screams back, sounding like a raging bonfire.

Oh.

"HOW CAN WE EXPECT OUR TRUE, GLOWING BEAUTY TO REALLY SHINE WHEN EVEN THE WALLS THEMSELVES GLOW HERE!" The blaze ignites, its flames lick the ceiling of the cavern.

"Uh…" you say. "Okay, I can make this better. If you just close your eyes I'll take you to—"

"No! No! No!" one of the other blazes says, also bursting into flames. "That's the last time that we take help from you! First, you come into our fortress and you insult us, and then you pretend you're going to help us and take us somewhere where we are ugly and dull! Clearly you are a devil come from the overworld to taunt us!"

"A devil?" you're confused now. *How did things get so bad so fast?* "No, I'm not a devil. If anything, you guys are the devils, right?"

The blazes stare at you angrily.

"Cause you live here in this place that's all on fire, and you're like on fire too and—" you try to explain.

"THAT'S IT!" one of the blazes screams.

Gordo starts to run, but you don't have time before the rain of fireballs comes down around you.

THE END

To go back to the last choice and try again, *turn to page 60. Or flip to the beginning and choose a new story!*

"I've got to find a portal that's been built already!" you say to yourself. "It's so simple! Some players are going to build a Nether portal anyways. If I can just find it, then I'm golden!"

The only question is: where? This is a big world. Who knows where there might be a nether portal...

You stare out at the darkness all around you. *If only there was a way to know which direction to start... like a glowing arrow or—*

Your jaw drops. *That's it! Glowing.*

You start running off towards a towering hill in the distance. As you run, you explain your genius out loud. "You can't just find obsidian anywhere! Obsidian only comes from lava. If you're wanting to build a Nether portal, you're going to need a bunch of obsidian and that means you'll have had to hang out near some lava recently. So, if you're looking for a nether portal, look near the lava! That's the easiest place to build them!"

And to make things even better, lava glows in the darkness. So, if you can get up somewhere high, you can just follow the glow. Reaching the summit of the tall hill, you look out hopefully. Besides the lights of the nearby village, the land around is all pitch black. No glows. No lava.

But you do see another big hill in the distance. You point yourself in its direction and start walking.

You don't have any luck there either, but as you crest the top of the third hill, your heart starts beating faster. There it is! A big orange glow flowing out onto the land just a couple hundred blocks away!

YES!

Without stopping for a second, you start running down the hill towards the glow. The lava isn't actually very far away. You only have to cross through this forest and forge through a small stream and you should be there. You're ecstatic and just feel like running. With your awkward, blocky zombie body, it ends up looking more like a demented gallup, but you're so happy that you don't even care. You traipse through the forest, so excited that you're hardly paying attention to where you're going. Your mind is absolutely fizzing with happiness and excitement: *I can't wait to get home! I'll get to see my parents again and my dog! Just think how good it will be to crawl into my own bed again! No more sleeping on the terrible, blocky cave floors! And this clothing, you can't even imagine how uncomfortable it is to wear pants that are all made out of blocks!*

I'm so glad that I just went alone. I didn't need any help. I'm perfectly fine all by myself—

A strange sensation grips you. It feels an awful lot like falling. You look down. Your feet aren't standing on anything. You see a cliff whizzing past beside you and then the sky fills your vision. You are definitely falling. You weren't paying attention and tripped right off the edge of a cliff and into…

You look down and see that same orange glow that you were so excited about early. Needless to say, you're not so excited to see the lake of lava as you plummet towards it.

Why didn't someone warn me? That's the last thought you have before you hit the lava with a gloopy splash. It has the same consistency as pudding. It's like pudding so hot that it melts your skin off in a second. *Terrible pudding…*

THE END

Too bad. But don't get discouraged. You should probably flip to the beginning and choose a new story.

"Hey, sorry," you say, "But I'm actually on a bit of a mission right now. I don't have time for this."

The pigman looks agitated, his eyes are darting around, not looking at you anymore.

"Though I do have a question for you," you continue. "Do you know where I might find a fort—"

In the middle of your sentence the zombie pigman takes off into the caves behind him.

"Oookaaaayyy," you say. " Nice to meet you too…"

You spin around to find Gordo. He's standing where you left him. He's leaning over and extending his tongue towards a block of Netherrack, just about to lick it.

"Don't do that!" you shout over at him, like you would at a young puppy trying to eat a shoe. "The stone is hot!"

You touch a nearby block to make a point and draw your hand back in a hurry as it almost burns your finger.

Gordo pauses, looks at you and then wanders over. "So what do we do now?" he asks.

You shrug. "I don't know. I guess we go back up to the bridge."

He looks over at the dangerous natural staircase that you took to get down here with a worried frown. "Back up there, eh?"

"Yeah," you say. "How about you go first and I'll be down here to catch you as you fall. Take your time."

Gordo agrees to the plan and begins to hop up the steep ledge of rocks while you watch from beneath him. You try really hard not to look at the glowing lava that waits below if he takes even one wrong step.

He's halfway there when you feel rumbling in the ground. *What's happening?* You spin around. There's a clamber of voices coming from the caves behind you. They sound like their groaning and… oinking.

Uh oh. You don't know why, but you're pretty sure you're in trouble.

"What's—" Gordo starts to ask but is immediately interrupted by the sight of zombie pigmen pouring out of the mouth of the cave just thirty blocks away from you.

"Climb!" you shout.

The pigmen are running straight towards you.

"It's real! It's real!" they're screaming. "He wasn't lying! The all-powerful zombie has come! What an amazing day! Look at me, zombie! Can I have an autoinkgraph, zombie?!"

You take a step backwards, up onto the rocky ledge that Gordo is climbing as the crowd gets closer. Then they're all around you, clambering to touch you, to speak to you.

You're overwhelmed by the noise, by the hoofs that are grabbing at you everywhere. You climb up one more block.

"DON'T GO, ZOMBIE!" one of the pigmen screams and several of them dive at you to pull you back down towards them.

Their hoofs strike you in the stomach, unbalancing you and sending you teetering backwards. You lose your footing, step back, but there's no block there.

You start to fall. As you do, the crowd suddenly grows quiet.

"Oops," one of the pigmen says.

Gordo and a hundred pigmen watch in complete silence as you plummet into the lava beneath and land with a sizzling splash.

THE END

To go back to the last choice and try again, *turn to page 38. Or flip to the beginning and choose a new story!*

"Open your eyes!" you chime happily.

The blazes do. They blink their eyes open, trying to take everything in. They look like newborn babies, first experiencing the world.

You put your hands on your hips. "How do you like it?" you ask. "Isn't it beautiful?"

The blazes seem to be staring mostly down at the lava sea that shines hotly from beneath you.

"Mmhm," you say, looking too. "It's pretty amazing!"

"No, it's not!" one of the blazes starts to scream, igniting into a flying fireball. "IT'S TOO BRIGHT!"

"Wha—" you say.

"THE LAVA IS BRIGHTER THAN ME!" the blaze screams.

"Yeah! ME TOO!" another one adds.

"WHAT AM I IF I'M NOT BRIGHT!" a third one cries.

This isn't good. You look back at Gordo for help, who looks like he's about to faint.

"ZOMBIE IS THIS WHAT YOU THINK HELPING LOOKS LIKE!?" the first blaze yells again.

"No, I— guys I was trying to help—"

"BY TAKING US SOMEWHERE WE HATE! WE ONLY GO OUT HERE WHEN WE *HAVE* TO! LIKE WHEN THERE'S A ZOMBIE THAT NEEDS ROASTING!"

"No, no, no, no—" you stammer, but there's no reasoning with them.

One second later you're a crispy order of zombie toast.

THE END

To go back to the last choice and try again, *turn to page 73. Or flip to the beginning and choose a new story!*

"Just exploring," you say. "It gets boring up there in the overworld so I thought I'd go see what else there was to see."

The blazes all stare at you, dumbstruck. "You… came… here?" one says.

You're confused. "Yeah? Why?"

"Well, this is the most boring place in the whole world! Trust us!"one of the blazes says, spinning quickly to emphasize his words.

"It's boring here?" you ask. "But what about all the lava and the fires and the walls that glow…"

"Out there, sure. But we don't like going out there. Even that stuff gets old pretty fast. No, we all stay inside the fortress mostly. Only each other for company and let me tell you, *that* gets old pretty fast too. Hang out with another blaze for eternity and they can get on your nerves pretty bad," the blaze says. The others shake their head and 'tsk, tsk.' It seems like they all agree. So much so that even talking about it has annoyed some of them. They drift out of the room haughtily… and hotly, come to think of it.

"Where's everybody… going?" you say as the blazes drift away from you. There's only three left in this room.

These guys are kind of grumps, you think. *I'm glad I don't have to hang out with them for too long. Just long enough to get me some blaze rods… but how?*

You think for a second and decide on the best way. Then you approach the blaze that you were talking to before and ask it a question.

If you ask it if you can have some blaze rods, *turn to page 72.*

If you ask it what annoys the blaze most about the other blazes, *turn to page 78.*

"…actually," you say, "I'm just a zombie that wandered through a Nether portal and happen to be here on a totally different quest. I'm not your leader or some sort of zombie pigman god. I'm just a regular old zombie."

"There's nothing regular about a zombie—" one of the pigmen starts to say.

"Yeah, there totally is," you cut him off. "Up there we're just like you down here. There's a whole bunch of us and we're not special at all. Sorry to burst your bubble. But if you think that zombies are gods, you're a bit crazy."

The pigmen just stare at you in disbelief.

"Come on, stop kneeling down," you shout, waving your arms.

They rise slowly and unsteadily.

"I actually could use your help," you say, "while you're here. I'm looking for a fortress, I need to find some blazes. Any idea which way I should go?"

The pigmen blink with confusion. "If we tell you… will you lead us?"

"No, guys," you say, "like I said, I'm just a normal old zombie."

The pigmen keep staring.

These guys are not helpful. You turn away from them and shepherd Gordo away, back into the cavern you came from.

"Thanks anyways," you call back. "Hope you have a great—" When you look over your shoulder, you realize the pigmen are gone.

Weird…

Gordo and you explore the larger cavern that the pigman lead you into in the first place. There are a couple offshoot passages, but none of them seem to go anywhere. In the middle of the cavern is a mysterious chunk of floating gravel that you stare at for a couple seconds.

You hear a rumbling and look around.

"Gordo," you say. "Do you hear that?"

"Wha—" Gordo listens. His giant nose scrunches up a bit. He hears it too.

It feels like the ground is shaking.

It's an earthquake? you think. *No sunlight, oceans of lava and now regular earthquakes? Can this place get any worse?*

You look up and realize that yes, yes it can. A horde of pigmen are running towards you from the cave where you met them before. But there aren't just four now. There are forty.

They keep pouring through the gap in the stone and extending into a circle around you and Gordo and the floating cube of gravel.

No, not forty: four hundred!

The last of them pour through the gap and take their place in the circle around you. The last zombie pigman is wearing a dark skull on top of his head and walks with importance. The circle breaks to let him through and he steps towards you.

"It's truuuuue," he says dramatically.

"Okay," you say putting up your hands. "I told you, I'm no god or leader or whatever… Just an average zombie—"

"You're not the return of the zombie that started the line of pigmen? The zombie that bit the first pig? Come here to judge us?" The skull-wearing pigman rudely interrupts.

"No," you say, "definitely not, I'm just—"

"It's not the all-powerful Zombie. It says it's not a god," the skull-wearing pigman interrupts again. "Then what must it be?" The pigman turns to the rest of the crowd.

You're confused. *What's happening here?*

The crowd seems confused too. They are silent.

But the leader pigman turns back to you and whispers loudly, "It's a demon!"

The pigmen go crazy and rush towards you.

You try to object, you try to explain, but it's too late. You're buried in a pile of angry zombie pigmen and there's no escape.

They grab you and lift you above their heads while you protest, and take you out of the cavern to the edge of the platform that hangs out over the lava ocean.

"Wait, wait, no—" you say, but they pay no attention.

In unison, they hurl you forward, out into the lava sea below.

As you fall, you catch a brief glimpse of Gordo standing near the edge waving to you. You raise your hand to wave back just as you hit the boiling surface of the lava.

THE END

To go back to the last choice and try again, *turn to page 80. Or flip to the beginning and choose a new story!*

"Hey," you say. "I really want to get out of your hair, but the only reason I'm here is that I need some blaze rods. About... six. Do you think I could have some? Any lying around?"

The blaze turns to look at you.

You wait. The blaze spins faster.

"Um," you say.

"WHAT DID YOU SAY?!" the blaze roars like a forest fire. The room fills with angry crackling. The other blazes are approaching and some are even coming in from the other room.

"Wait... I don't know..." You think back through what you asked to see what could have angered them. Slapping your forehead, figuring it out. "Oh! I meant: Could I have some blaze rods, *please.*"

This only seems to make them madder. Now, you're surrounded by all seven blazes, in a tight circle all around you. They're all spinning faster and faster and crackling angrily.

"It's nice to see you all getting along," you say quietly, trying to put a nice spin on things.

"BLAZE RODS!" one of them yells right in your face. "ONLY COME! FROM DEAD BLAZES!" A sinking feeling fills your stomach.

"YOU HAVE ASKED US TO DIE!"

You swallow hard. You didn't know, it was just a mistake. You didn't mean any wrong. But they don't know that and they're not letting you off easy. All of them ignite at once, their spinning bodies wreathed in flames.

"WHAT DO YOU HAVE TO SAY FOR YOURSELF!" one bellows.

If you say that you didn't know and tell them to take it easy, *turn to page 53.*

If you apologize profusely, *turn to page 56.*

"Hey guys," you say. "Will you do something for me? I promise, *promise*, that it's going to help. If you do what I tell you, you'll never be bored again!"

The blazes seem curious. "What is iiittt…" one of them asks.

"I need you all to close your eyes." You clasp your hands together and pray that they'll do it. Some of them seem sceptical, but one of the blazes clamps his eyes shut and then, one by one, the others do the same.

"Okay, hold hands and—" you start to say.

The blazes don't do anything and you realize your mistake. *No hands.*

"Uh, never mind, just follow my voice, okay?" You start walking to the door and the blazes float after you dreamily with their eyes closed.

You pass through the darker room you came from. "This way!" you say. "Keep those eyes closed."

You reach the door out to the ledge beyond. "Okay, come on out here, careful of the door and don't go too far from the wall, the ledge is nar—"

One of the blazes shoots out the door and off the side of the ledge.

"Ah!" you scream.

But it doesn't fall. It just hangs right where it is.

"Oh, right," you say. "Flying, handy."

You turn around and see Gordo staring at you with the biggest eyes you've ever seen. This is clearly a nightmare for him: a zombie leading seven blazes out onto a thin ledge over an ocean of vicious lava. It wasn't a good day for Gordo.

"What are you—" Gordo starts, but you just put your finger over your lips.

You turn around to the blazes and open your mouth.

If you tell them to open their eyes, *turn to page 67.*

If you lead them across the thin bridge, *turn to page 60.*

Easy, you think to yourself. *Just because I can't mine obsidian doesn't mean I can't get some. There's got to be a town nearby here that has a merchant which can sell me some.*

You look around and the wilderness around you. *The only question is where…*

For a second, you really wish that you had someone to help you. Maybe you should have taken Madame Mole's help after all.

No, no, you say to yourself sternly. *I can do this by myself! I've done everything else by myself. All it take is a little thinking…*

You spy a nearby mountain and head right for it, walking as quick as you can. When you get there you climb up a little ways until you have a good view of the surrounding countryside.

In the darkness all around you, you see exactly what you're looking for: the lights of another village not too far from the village that you just left. You take a second to commit to memory how to get there and then head out with a smug smile on your face.

You wander through a forest and along a stream for a little ways, waving at some other zombies as you pass them. After a couple minutes of walking, you break through the trees and feel a burst of excitement. A large field spreads out in front of you, but that's not what's exciting. No, it's the lights at the other side of the field that have set your heart beating faster.

You found the town and you didn't need anyone's help to do it! *See Madame Mole, I told you I was fine,* you think as you jog across the field.

There are a couple villagers standing around at the edge of the town. *What are they doing up at this time of night,* you ponder, as you approach one of them.

"Hey," you say as you get close.

The villager turns and his eyes bug out of his head. "He— wha— who goes there?!" he shouts, stepping closer to get a better look.

You extend your hand towards him. "Hello, my name's—"

"ALERT! ALERT! ALERT!" he starts shouting.

"Wha—" You feel offended.

"ZOMBIE ALERT!" the villager yells.

Oh... right.

Villagers start pouring out of their houses and rushing towards you with torches and wooden swords.

You turn to escape, but the villagers are coming fast. Now you realize it was silly to have approached the village alone. If only you'd had a villager with you to go into the town for you...

The screaming of the villagers gets louder as you run and then you feel a solid *thwack* on your head as a wooden sword strikes you. In a second, you're surrounded. It's all over.

THE END

Too bad. But don't get discouraged. You should probably flip to the beginning and choose a new story.

"We've been looking in the wrong place the whole time!" you shout and Gordo covers his ears. "Think about it, what are Nether portals made out of?"

Gordo shrugs. "Black stuff?"

"No— Well, yeah, kinda, obsidian, which is black stuff. And where does obsidian come from?" You jump to your feet.

He stares at the ceiling as if he's trying to remember an answer on a test. "An obsidian farm?"

"Ye— No. You really don't know a lot about anything, do you?" you groan.

He shakes his head.

Well, at least he knows that he doesn't know anything…

"Anyways," you continue. "Obsidian comes from lava, when it meets water. So if players are going to build a portal they will probably build it near lava, where they just got the resources. Come on, let's go," you say.

As you head out of the cave you turn back. "Oh wait, do you know where there are any flows of lava nearby?"

Gordo's mouth hangs open dumbly. You realize your mistake. *He doesn't know anything.* "Forget I asked that. Let's get going."

The good thing about searching for lava in the nighttime is that it glows. If there's any around, it's going to be visible for hundreds of blocks in every direction. You try to get up to some tall places and look out. The first couple hilltops don't give you anything, but when you climb up a tall sand dune, you see a deep orange glow coming from the north and your undead heart jumps in your undead chest.

You run off, dragging Gordo behind you. You're so excited as you go, that you're hardly paying attention to where you're going. Thoughts are just fizzing around your mind: *I can't wait to see my family! I can't wait to be home in my bed!*

"ROTNEY!"

Your day dream is shattered. You come back to the world around you and stop walking, startled. At first, you're angry at Gordo for startling you, but then you look down...

Your left foot is hovering in the air over a giant lake of lava. You were just about to step off the side of a cliff and tumble to a fiery death. Quickly, you scamper back and take a couple huge breaths.

Turning to the little villager, you smile wide. "Thank goodness for you Gordo! Man, without you I'd be burnt rotten flesh right now! I owe you everything Gordo!"

He looks like he doesn't know what to say.

"Your grandmother was right! I did need your help!" you blush.

Gordo's huge nose turns bright red. Clearly, you're embarrassing him. You decide to drop the issue and get back to searching, though your heart doesn't stop beating hard.

You complete a tour around the lava lake and don't see any portals, but just as you're about to go around again, you spot a couple players down near the surface of the lake with a couple buckets. One has a diamond axe.

This is exactly what you were looking for! They pour some water on the lava and start mining it away with a diamond axe. You're giddy with excitement as you watch the two players collect the black stone and then wander away from the lava pool. They go around a little hill and you can't see them anymore. *You could be losing your only chance!*

You start running after them and Gordo tries to grab at you. "You've got to be careful man!"

You look at him sceptically.

If you run after them right away, *turn to page 109.*

If you follow Gordo's advice, *turn to page 92.*

"Hey. These other guys really get on your nerves?" you say with a friendly tone. "Tell me, what's the thing that annoys you *the most*.. Get it off your chest."

He turns to you. The blaze looks a little sceptical. "Why do you care?"

"I don't know," you shrug, glancing at him sideways. "Sometimes it's just good to talk about these things. Makes it feel better."

The blaze thinks about that and must agree, because a second later it says, "What annoys me the most? Probably Spark, she's in the other room, and boy does she think she's the best. She's always got to fly the highest and glow the brightest. She's always letting you know that she's spinning the fastest. Like, *no one cares!*"

You nod, as if you totally agree and have felt that way about Spark for your whole life. "Why do you think that *really* bothers you?' you ask.

"Well," says the blaze, "'cause it's not true of course! Like, she thinks she's all that, but does she even notice the other blazes who do fly the highest or spin the fastest? No!"

You have an idea. "And you, I mean you're one of those blazes right. So, it's not even fair."

The blaze looks at you and a fire lights in your eyes. "Yeah! Exactly! Nobody even sees what I do, 'cause I'm not showing off all the time. Not fair at all… You really understand—" The blaze pauses. "What's your name?"

"Rotney," you say, offering your zombie name.

"Rotney. You really get me. Thanks, man. I'm Ember, by the way."

You extend your hand to Ember. "Pleasure to meet you."

He just stares at it. *Right,* you realize, *no hands.* Ember floats around a little, looking more relaxed after your conversation. You still don't have any blaze rods.

If you go to the other room to talk to Spark, *turn to page 99.*

If you attack Ember for his blaze rod, *turn to page 84.*

"Wait, I have a question," you say. "Why do you guys stay in here all the time, anyways? Is there a reason?"

"Is there a *reason!*" the blaze exclaims. The other blazes laugh. "Duh."

"B-but why? What's the reason?" you ask.

"Really? You don't know?" the blaze says suspiciously.

You shake your head honestly.

"It's bright out there!" says the blaze as if it were the most obvious thing.

You look around at the other blazes that are watching now. "You— you guys don't like the light? But you're fiery things—"

"No," says the blaze suddenly. "We're not scared of light. We just don't like being outshone. We want to be the brightest thing! Otherwise what makes us special?"

"Oh," you say. *These guys are so full of themselves,* you think. *But then we're all different...*

You realize that if you could get them out of the fortress, they wouldn't be so bored anymore...

If you ask the blazes to close their eyes and follow you, *turn to page 73*.

If you just go get some overworld stuff and bring it back, *turn to page 86*.

"Sure, okay," you say. "But one condition, I've got this villager with me." You point back at Gordo, who is licking a nearby piece of netherrack. "You promise not to eat him?"

The pigman throws one look in Gordo's direction. "Oh yeah. He's cool?"

"He's cool…" you say sceptically.

"Then no biggie, he can come too!"

You wave Gordo over and start to follow the pigman into the nearby cave. Gordo trots up beside you holding his tongue. "It'th hot," he says.

You just shake your head and suppress a smile.

The pigman takes a hard right and you see three other pigman standing in a echoey netherrack cave. He runs off to greet them while you watch carefully.

He points at you and the other zombie pigmen look. They all start running over at once.

"I don't feel good about this," you say, taking the smallest step back. By the way that Gordo's hiding behind you, you guess he's not feeling great about it either.

When the zombie pigmen are just a couple steps away, they slow and then stop, staring at you the whole time. Then all at once, all three of them drop to their knees and bow their heads.

What in the Nether?… you think to yourself.

The pigman that lead you there drops to his knee as well.

"Okay, what's going on here?" you ask. "What's with all the bowing?"

When the pigmen hear your voice, they gasp and bow their heads even lower.

"Won't someone talk to me?!" you howl.

"Yes, moinkst honoured guest," the first pigman oinks and groans, raising his head. "We bow because we want to show you our great thankfulness for having come here!"

"I didn't come here for you guys…" you say wryly.

One of the other pigmen pops up their head and talks in a high-pitched squeal. "But why did you come here at all! Your kind doink't belong here. Zombies," the pigman says the word in a whisper, "doink't exist here in the Nether. *You* come from the *Overworld…*"

"Oooooo," gasp the other pigmen.

You roll your eyes. *These guys are a bit nutty. Probably comes from having a pig brain in their skull.*

"But we knoink why you've come," says the first pigman again. "You've come down to save us. Magically descended from the heavens to lead our people and show us the way!"

Oh boy, these guys are not right in their pig heads.

"Well…" you say trying to think of what to do. You take a deep breath.

If you say you're here to lead them, *turn to page 57*.

If you correct them, *turn to page 69*.

You rub your toe into the ground. "No, it's fine, you can stay chief."

The crowd groans, clearly upset and the chief looks quite smug.

"Very well!" the chief screams. "I have been chosen to lead by the zombie. Now, we must prepare to make our holy guest comfortable. Guards, make sure the zombie and his angel are comfortable!" When she says 'angel' she gestures at Gordo.

You look back at him and squint. *Angel? That's the weirdest looking angel I've ever seen.* Even Gordo seems to be a bit confused.

A couple pigmen gather around the chief. Another twenty or so pigmen come over and stand around you in a circle.

You settle in and watch as the chief whispers some commands and hundreds of pigmen start moving gravel around the island.

Curious, you sidle over to one of the pigmen and nudge them. "Hey, what's going on?"

"We're building you a temple, zombie!" the pigman says respectfully.

"Oh, that's nice," you say. You shout over at Gordo. "They're building me a temple."

This doesn't make him look any less worried. You go over to his spot within the circle of guards and sit down beside him.

"What's wrong?" you ask.

He shrugs. "I don't know— I— I guess I'm just a scaredy cat."

You watch as the pigmen finish building a giant pyramid and then start stacking netherrack blocks on top of it, making a small room.

You turn to Gordo. "No, what is it? You can tell me."

"It's just," he mumbles. "I know these guards are supposed to be protecting us, but it just kind of feels like we're prisoners."

You stare around you at the guards. You squish up your face, thinking: *No, that's crazy… Right?*

The chief cuts through the circle and with her loudest voice says. "Zombie! We have built a temple for you, will you grace it with your presence?"

You smile. "Sure," you say. It seems fun.

The pigmen guards lead you to the base of the pyramid and walk up it with you while the crowd cheers. At the top, the chief gestures to the little room of netherrack built on top of the pyramid and says, "Zombie, this is your sacred chamber. Is it fit for you?"

A little opening for a door has been left on the side of the box of netherrack. You step inside and Gordo follows you. It's small, and there's nothing special about it, but you have to admit that this is the coolest house that you've ever had in Minecraft. It was actually *built* by zombie pigmen. *What's cooler than that?*

You turn around and start saying, "Yeah, this will be gr—"

A pigman is putting a block of netherrack in the door.

"Wait!" you scream, but then the second block is placed and the room is sealed. Only the slight glow of the netherrack lights the room. "Let me out!"

You swing your hands at the wall, but netherrack is too hard to be dug with anything but a pickaxe. You burn yourself with every pounding against the wall. Gordo starts crying softly.

"This way, the zombie will be with us forever!" the chief yells from outside. And then much quieter, she whispers through the walls. "And he'll never challenge my power again…"

THE END

To go back to the last choice and try again, *turn to page 57.* Or *flip to the beginning and choose a new story!*

This is your moment, you realize. You've lulled the blaze into feeling comfortable with you, even liking you. He thinks you're friends, which makes it the perfect moment to betray him.

He'll never expect it.

Ember drifts into the corner and you take a quick look over your shoulder. There are two other blazes in the room, but they're over in the far corners. Ember is alone. You know that if you're going to do it, you have to do it now.

And you're doing it…

It's a little tricky to figure out how to attack a blaze. You see, they don't really have a body so much. They have a head, but the rest of them is just spinning bars and smoke. You decide that the head is the best place to aim for.

You take a couple quick steps up to the blaze and swing your fist right for the little head floating on top of the chaos of smoke and spinning bars. You close your eyes instinctively and are pleased as you feel the impact against your green fist. You hit!

And then one of the blaze's bars swings around and hits you in the side of the arms, sending you spinning. You're already off balance as the blaze turns around to face you.

"What was—" Ember starts.

But you don't let him finish. You steady yourself a little and aim for the "body" of the blaze, because that's all you can reach. You shoot your fist into the centre of the plume of smoke and hit… nothing.

But the spinning bars hit you. One smacks you right in the arm. *That's going to bruise.*

You stagger back, your arm smarting.

Ember starts making a horrible sound. It's a whooshing and a snapping, like breaking bones and a hurricane.

"WHAT ARE YOU DOING?!" the blaze roars. He immediately lights on fire.

There's no point in waiting any longer. Every second that passes just makes things more and more dangerous. You go for it. Aiming for his head this time, you swing your fist.

You hit, but you're not sure that it's a victory. You pull back your fist... and it's on fire.

Oh boy.

You wave your fist awkwardly in the air, trying to put it out, but it seems to just be making it worse, spreading the flames further and further down your arm.

The living pillar of fire rises further and further into the air, crackling and snapping.

You decide that you might be losing this fight and you turn to run—

You stop in your tracks. There are two other blazes, on fire and floating in the air, right behind you. You make a dash for the door. You take a couple steps and then dance back as the ground in front of you suddenly erupts in flames.

They don't want you to escape.

The four other blazes drift into the room. One is flying a little higher and a little faster than the others.

Spark really is *annoying,* you think. And funnily enough, that's the last thought you ever have because the next second, the air fills with fire.

THE END

To go back to the last choice and try again, *turn to page 78. Or flip to the beginning and choose a new story!*

"You got it! I'll be right back!" you say loudly to the blaze. It turns around and watches you as you march proudly out of the room and then out of the fortress. As you go through the door that leads back onto the ledge, you nearly run into Gordo who is waiting just outside the door.

"What are you doing out here?" you ask, slipping past him.

"I— uh— I was scared to go after you. I heard some weird noises in there…" Gordo stammers.

"Yeah!" you say, leading the way along the ledge. Gordo follows you like a baby duckling. "I found some blazes!"

"You did?" Gordo asks, with excitement bubbling in his voice.

"Mmhmm!" You slow down as you reach the thin bridge that you took to get there and tiptoe across it carefully.

"So, we're done! We're going home! Oh my mods! Thank goodness!" Gordo is so happy that he doesn't even realize that he's walking across the tiny bridge that he hates.

"Well, not exactly," you say. "We're going back up there, but we have to come back. I want to bring the blazes cool things from up above."

"Oh…" Gordo is clearly disappointed. He looks down at his feet and realizes he's hundreds of blocks over an ocean of lava with only one block of netherrack keeping him from falling in. "Ooohhhhh…" he moans.

You get to the other side and impatiently tap your foot, waiting for Gordo to cross slowly and shakily.

He finally makes it across and the two of you take off again through the cavern on the other side.

"So we have to get things from home and bring them back, and then we'll get the blaze rods and be able to go home?" Gordo asks as he jogs to keep up with you.

"Uh… no actually." You stop in front of the portal and after taking a deep breath, plunge right in. "Actually, I kind of—"

Your voice gets sucked out of your mouth when the whole world turns purple and a hook behind your belly button yanks you into a different world.

You're back in the overworld, back where it's normal, and the cool darkness of the air is comforting. When Gordo pops through the portal behind you, you continue.

"—Offended the blazes by demanding their dead bodies, they were going to roast me alive, but I promised I'd help them to make it up."

Gordo staggered dizzily out of the portal. "So we're not going to get the blaze rods?"

"Guess not, not yet," you say, crudely digging up some grass. "Grab that flower over there," you say.

You wander over to a couple trees and take down some leaves, and pick up a little sapling that drops onto the grass. That's when you notice a bucket under one of the trees.

"My lucky day!" you say, grabbing it and scooping some water from a nearby stream.

You stride back to the portal and making sure that Gordo and the flower are following you, you jump back in.

The two of you walk all the way back to the fortress in silence. You think that maybe Gordo is annoyed that you had to come back.

Soon, you're striding back into the room of blazes, with Gordo reluctantly following you.

"Tada! I'm back!" you say. "And I have many mysterious wonders from the overworld!"

The blazes are immediately interested. They gather around, spinning faster than normal.

"For my first trick," you proclaim. "The strange, beautiful overworld thing called grass! This is everywhere on the ground up there!"

You take the block grass and with a flourish of your hand you smack it onto the ground. "TADA!"

The blazes are looking, but they don't seem impressed. You follow their gaze, looking down. The grass on the ground is a dead-looking brown colour…

"So, it's like fuzzy netherrack?" one of the blazes says. "I thought the overworld was better than that…"

This is doing nothing to help their boredom…

"No, no, no!" you say. "It is! It is! Look, this strange thing is like a mushroom, but more colourful and green and much more delicate and beautiful… The Flower!" You wave at Gordo and he places his flower on the ground.

It is immediately wilted, brown, and foul smelling.

"Zombies have a strange idea of beauty," one of the blazes comments. A couple of them lose interest and start to drift away.

"No!" you say. "Okay that didn't work, but trees are much sturdier, trees will survive and amaze you!"

"I've heard of trees!" one blaze says.

"Yes! And now you'll see one!" You smack the sapling onto the block of wilted grass.

It immediately catches fire.

"*That's* a tree?" one of the blazes asks sceptically. "We have those all over the place, here! We call them fire…"

You shake your head.

"I thought you were going to help us," one of the blazes says, "but you've just made me much more bored. I thought there were beautiful things out there, but they're all just like what we have here. The world's soooo boring. Thanks zombie…" It starts spinning, and getting a little angry. The others follow suit.

"No! No!" you say. "I've got something really special. If this works, you'll forgive me, right?"

"Sure," one of the blazes says sceptically. "What is it…"

"Water!" You swing out the bucket and splash it into the air.

It immediately turns to steam and floats off.

"Dangit!" you mumble.

"What is this zombie! Did you want to make us more depressed!" a blaze yells. "This was terrible!" It lights on fire.

You turn to run, but you're too slow. The fireballs start flying before you can reach the door.

Your last thought is: *Burning zombie flesh doesn't smell very good…*

THE END

To go back to the last choice and try again, *turn to page 97. Or flip to the beginning and choose a new story!*

You gasp a deep breath, gather your courage and head towards the knife-thin bridge.

"Oh come on," Gordo says behind you. "Really!?"

You turn around with a laugh. "What?!"

"Do you always have to choose just the most dangerous option?!" Gordo says with exasperation. You've never heard him talk like this before, and it makes you giggle. He smiles and in a groaning, sing-song voice, he says, "Oh, I know what looks fun, let's walk across this tiny bridge over the biggest pool of lava ever. What a great way to spend an afternoon!"

He's mocking you, but it's hilarious. When you stop laughing you just shrug. "We've gotta go this way," you say. "That big block right there, isn't it a tad suspicious?"

Gordo stares at the roughly box-shaped protrusion of rock coming down from the ceiling. "Everything's made of blocks in *this* world Rotney, or did you forget?"

"What's gotten into you!" you say with a smile. "No, I know it's made of blocks, but it's kind of rectangular. Look around, that's not a normal rock formation. There's a fortress in there, I know it."

And with that you charge across the bridge, keeping your eyes on your feet, but trying not to look at the lava far below. It's tricky.

Gordo screams all the way across the bridge. "AHHHHHHHHHHHHHH!"

You reach the other side and take a deep breath, walking to safe ground on a little platform connected to the mysterious giant rock box.

"AAAAHHHHHHHHHHHHH!"

You turn to Gordo. "Shh, shh, look down."

He does and notices that he's safely on the other side of the bridge, standing on a fairly wide part of the platform. "AHHHHH—oh."

"Yeah," you punch him in the arm and then spin around to examine your surroundings. The platform extends off to your right for a ways and you follow it with Gordo trailing you.

Soon you come to a door that cuts through the rock into the inside of the giant stone block. The ledge does extend further along the block and turns the corner. You can't see how far it goes.

If you go through the door, *turn to page 55*.

If you keep following the ledge, *turn to page 51*.

He did save me from the lava. Maybe there's more to this guy than I know... you think. *Maybe I should listen to him.*

Reluctantly, you follow Gordo's advice and stop running.

"Okay, we'll do this slowly," you say and together, you and Gordo creep up towards the hill that the players have disappeared behind. You keep your ears peeled for any noises, but you hear nothing. Maybe your ears are rotting more than you thought... Or maybe the players have already run off and they're far away...

You get to the hill and are about to go around the other side when Gordo grabs your arm again.

"What now?" you ask, a little ruder than you have to. "Are you scared about what might be on the other side?"

He pouts a little. "No." And then he smiles. "But I could see why you'd think that..."

You laugh softly, "Yeah."

"No, it's not that," he says. "I just had an idea!"

He says it like this has never happened to him before. You try to keep your face straight and look like you're listening carefully.

"I should go first," he says.

You squint at him. "You're the brave one now?"

"No, no," he says. "It's just that I'm a villager, if the players see me, they'll just be a little confused. But if they see you first, well, you know... it could get bad."

"Chop, chop, chop time," you say nodding. "That's a good point. I hadn't thought of that."

Gordo clears his throat, does a weird little shake and then starts to sneak around the hill.

Maybe he does know a thing or two, you think as you watch him disappear.

It's hard to wait patiently. You fidget and walk in circles. Then you hear loud booming voices from the other side of the hill. *Players.* You can't make out what they're saying at first but luckily, like every player, their words all appear up in the sky above their heads. You back up a little so that you can read them over the top of the hill.

"HEY LOOK A MOB!" one of them says.

"I GOT IT!" says the other.

"WAIT…"

"WAIT! THAT'S A VILLAGER! IS THERE A VILLAGE NEAR HERE?"

"HAVEN'T SEEN ONE… WEIRD."

"IS THIS A NEW UPDATE TO THE GAME? IS THIS LIKE AN ENDERMAN IN DISGUISE OR SOMETHING? I'M GOING TO TAKE IT OUT JUST IN CASE!"

You ball your hands into cube-shaped fists and start marching around the hill. And then you see the next line:

"WAIT! YOU CAN'T KILL A VILLAGER, MAN."

"WHY NOT?!"

"BAD LUCK, EVERYONE KNOWS THAT. DO YOU WANT HEROBRINE FOLLOWING YOU EVERYWHERE YOU GO?"

"…" says the other. "FINE. WHATEVER."

You stop holding your breath.

"BACK TO WORK."

A couple minutes later, Gordo reappears around the hill. He has the biggest smile on. "We've got it," whispers. "Come on."

You follow him around the hill and just as you reach the other side, he puts his hand out to stop you. He goes forward a couple steps and then waves you over.

You come around the hill just in time to see the two players disappear into a newly built Nether portal. The weird, purple barrier gobbles both of them up and they snap out of existence.

You jump for joy. "Yus! You did great little dude!" you shout.

He smiles. "So are we going to go in?"

"Just give it a second. We don't want to pop out the other side and find ourselves surrounded by players."

You wait a couple anxious minutes and then when you've decided that enough time has passed, you walk up to the purple portal.

You look back at Gordo. He looks absolutely petrified.

"Ready?" you ask.

He shakes his head.

"Come on." You grab his hand and step into the portal.

Turn to page 35 to go through the portal.

"We're going to go to the nearest merchant!" you say. "You know of a good trader near here? Maybe in one of the villages nearby?"

Gordo's eyes open so wide that you're worried that *they'll* fall out too.

"Me?" he asks.

You make a point of looking all around the two of you. There's a couple trees, two very big rocks and one sheep chewing on grass behind you. "No, I was asking the sheep," you say sarcastically.

Gordo sighs. "Oh good!" he says, relieved.

"No!" you shout, exasperated. "I was talking to you, of course! Sheep can't talk."

"I dunno," Gordo says quietly. "Until today, I didn't think that zombies could talk either."

He's got a good point...

"Okay, anyways, yeah I was asking you," you say, brushing it off. "You grew up in the area. Is there a villager merchant in the area that might sell some obsidian?"

Gordo thinks. You can tell, because his eyes cross just slightly.

You wait patiently, tapping your foot against the hard packed dirt.

You are just starting to worry that maybe he's glitched out or something when he breaks the silence with a "Yes!"

"There's a merchant at the next village over... She's got all sorts of things. Probably some obsidian. Don't know, but probably!" Gordo smiles a little, which you realize you've never seen him do yet.

"Sounds great," you say, getting a little impatient. "Lead the way!"

There's silence for a second.

"Me?" Gordo asks.

You bury your head in your hands.

A couple minutes later, you've finally convinced Gordo that yes, in fact, he's the one who should be leading the way, and the two of you are weaving through a forest towards the neighbouring village. Gordo gets lost a couple times, but luckily you're paying attention and each time he strays from the path, you're able to help him retrace your steps.

It's a struggle, but soon you're standing at the edge of the forest, staring at the village that is lit up on the horizon.

"That's it!" Gordo says excitedly.

Finally, you think and charge forward towards the town. You've got to make up for all that dilly-dallying in the woods.

"Wait! Wait!" Gordo shouts. "Rotney!" His timid little voice calls to you from behind.

What is it now?, you wonder. The town is calling you and you don't want to waste any more time.

If you stop and listen to Gordo, *turn to page 20.*

If you hurry to the village, *turn to page 18.*

You eye one of the blazes who has wandered into the corner and is staring up at the wall. You think for a second, watching another blaze leave the room and then you approach the one by the wall.

"Excuse me," you say.

It whirls around in a crack of sparks. "Mmhmm," it says lazily.

"I was just wondering if there's anything that particularly bothers you right now. Like, is there anything on your nerves or getting you down…"

The blaze thinks for a second, spins and then simply says, "No," and drifts further into the corner.

You chew on your lip, and then take another step after it and ask. "Okay, well maybe not, but is there anything that you'd like? Do you have any wishes? Like, pretend I'm a genie!"

The blaze turns and gives you a long look up and down. "You don't look like a genie…"

"Okay, forget that," you say folding your arms awkwardly over your chest.

"You're supposed to have flowing pants and a cool hat. Also, where's your lamp—"

You cut the blaze off. "Never mind, is there anything that you'd like?"

The blaze shrugs sadly. "I don't know. I can't really think of anything. I'm just kind of bored of everything?"

"You're bored?" you say too excitedly. *This might be something you can help!*

"Uhuh," says the blaze. "Nothing ever happens in here, inside the fortress—"

"Oh yeah, you guys never leave… right."

"Yeah, duh, so I don't know. It would be great if we saw something new once in a while that wasn't some bricks, netherrack, fire, or a couple wither skeletons…" The blaze trails off, thinking.

You're thinking too.

"Oh! I know," the blaze exclaims. "You're from the overworld, right? I'm sure you've seen tons of exciting wonderful things up there! I'd love to have some of those in here. That's what I wish!"

"For some overworld things here, inside your fortress?"

The blaze nods. "I mean… if you really want to help…"

You nod forcefully. "I do!"

"Well then…" The blaze drifts off again, leaving you alone.

You contemplate for a second. There's something nagging at the back of your mind.

If you go to bring some overworld things to the blazes, *turn to page 86.*

If you ask the blaze why they never leave the fortress, *turn to page 79.*

Patience, you tell yourself. You've got the inkling of a plan.

You sneak away from Ember, who is quite content floating around in the corner and tiptoe through the door that the other blazes disappeared into.

The door leads to a balcony looking out over a much bigger chamber. A staircase extends down from the balcony to the floor of the cavern below. Off in the distance is a door leading off to another room.

More interesting to you are the blazes who are floating in the air nearby. Most of the blazes are hanging our around the balcony and they're watching you carefully. But one of the blazes is flying in the middle of the chamber, near the ceiling, far from the balcony.

You have a feeling you know which blaze is Spark…

You go to the edge of the balcony and shout over at the faraway blaze. "Hey, Spark! Spark! Are you Spark?"

The blaze looks at you with shock in its eyes and then slowly drifts towards you. You can't help but notice that it's spinning *very* fast.

"How do you… know my name?" the blaze says.

So I was right, you think.

"Oh, some of the other blazes in there were talking and mentioned your name… the rest was a lucky guess," you say.

"Okay…" There seems to be a question in her eyes, but she doesn't say it. "So, what can I help you with?"

"Oh, I don't know, I was just curious whether there was anyone in particular who got on your nerves around here?" you ask innocently.

"What?" says Spark. "No, everyone's fine. I like everyone here and everyone likes me!" She smiles and spins quickly.

"I don't know about that…" you mumble. "But whatever—"

"Wait, what?" Spark crackles, suddenly quiet.

"Oh forget it," you say, pretending you didn't mean to let it slip. "It's nothing..."

"No, you said that... does someone *not* like me?" Spark asks. "Be honest."

You frown and look down at your shoes. "Well, Ember just said something, I'm sure it doesn't mean anything..."

She waits for you to continue.

"He just mentioned that he thought you were a bit of a... show-off. I don't know. His words!" you say, shrugging your shoulders.

She looks hurt. A little burst of flame explodes from her shoulder. Well, she doesn't have shoulders. But, it's about where a shoulder would be.

"I'm not a show-off," she says quietly.

"Well, maybe that's not quite what he said," you say, pretending to think. "He said that you think you fly the highest and glow the brightest when really it's him, right?"

"No!" she shouts, fire lighting up all around her. "He's definitely not even close to the best flyer or the brightest glower. Flash, over there," she nods at a blaze floating nearby to her right, "she's probably the best, even glows better than me. And Roast," she nods at a blaze on her left, "if anyone can rival me in flying, it's him. But definitely not Ember! That guy's the worst!"

You bite your lip. Things are starting to work the way you wanted...

If you tell Spark to go confront Ember, *turn to page 30*.

If you make trouble with Flash and Roast, *turn to page 106*.

You clear your throat.

"Yes!" you shout. "I have a message for you as your creator! As *the zombie!*"

You think quickly. The crowd is giving you their whole attention. No one is making a peep.

"I have come to warn you!" you shout. "About a grave danger! Something that threatens the lives of all pigmen here in the Nether."

The silence of the crowd makes you smile slightly and then you curve your lips down into a grimace. "The blazes!" you shout. "They will end this beautiful community of pigmen that I started and so I have come to warn you. Together, we have to stop them!"

Slowly, one of the pigmen steps forward and bows low. "Supreme zombie, sir, may I ask a question?"

You nod.

"Th-the blazes, they never leave their foinkrtresses, they've never bothered us before, how will they end us all?" The pigman skitters back into the crowd.

You straighten up. "They've never bothered you... yet. But that will change! Soon, they will be all over here, throwing fireballs and burning everything to a crisp."

The pigmen gasp.

"Wh-wh-what can we do to stop them?" the same pigman asks cautiously.

You pretend to think for a second. "Well, I suppose we have to end them before they end us. We have to go to war!"

The crowd is silent, and you start to worry. *Is this not going to work?* And then the pigmen erupt into cheers. "To war!" they shout.

They all go immediately to work, gathering their golden swords and getting ready. In just a couple minutes, you find a perfectly arrayed pigman army standing in front of you. It's astonishing.

One of the pigmen steps forward. "We're ready to go, great zombie. Will you lead us?"

You stare at them for a second. "Of course!"

You march down from the altar and through the army of pigmen towards the bridge. The army follows you. They march in a pretty orderly fashion for a bunch of undead pigs. You're impressed.

As you march, one of the pigmen gives you directions to the nearest fortress. You find yourself marching back through some familiar caverns and then emerging again on the same platform where you met the first pigmen. Looking down at the lava below, you hop and jump up the escarpment. A couple of the pigmen carry Gordo up the uneven rock steps.

You keep marching across the thin bridge you first noticed with hundreds of pigmen following you. For a second, you're worried if the bridge can handle that weight. But the whole army makes it across and you weave through a couple caves until you enter a chamber made of bricks. You're inside the fortress…

It doesn't take long before you find the blazes. You spot them from afar on a platform high over the chamber you're in. You turn to your army and yell, "Attack!"

The pigmen race forward towards the blazes. You take a couple steps back. You don't want to be right up in the face of the blazes. *You* know that they can be pretty dangerous. *Way* more dangerous than a pigman. But then again, you have four hundred pigmen. You can afford to lose a couple. And then, at the end… you just have to go pick up those blaze rods.

You smile a little watching the pigmen charge towards the stairs that lead up to the blazes.

But the blazes turn to notice the sea of pigmen rushing towards them and start firing fireballs from their platform. The first fireball strikes a pigman, who immediately explodes into dust.

Woah!

The rest of the blazes come to the edge of the platform and start hurling fireballs. The pigmen are melting away under the attack. Every time one of them gets close to the stairs, it gets blown up.

The blazes take to the air and start hurling even more fireballs. Pigmen are getting roasted all over the place. Luckily more pigmen keep charging past you into the fray.

Your smile dulls a little bit.

The blazes lower themselves over the pigman army so they can strike even faster. The air is filled with terrifying oinks.

And then... you realize there aren't any more pigmen charging past you.

"Come on," you shout. "Army! Charge!"

There's no response. You turn around. There's no army behind you.

Your army is a pile of roasted pork and bones scattered all around you.

The last terrified oink fills the air and you look up.

With nothing left to burn, the blazes are coming towards *you*.

You yelp and try to run.

But you can't outrun a fireball.

THE END

To go back to the last choice and try again, *turn to page 3. Or flip to the beginning and choose a new story!*

You glance sideways at the blazes. None of them seem to really be watching you. But it *is* hard to tell when they keep spinning around like that.

You decide to take the chance, and calmly, casually, just walk towards the door.

No one says anything.

No one stops you.

You're a couple steps from the door and you're almost home free. You just pretend that you're not doing anything wrong, that everything's totally normal and a couple more steps, and…

You're free. You're out of the blazes' chamber and into the darker room that you came through earlier. Keeping your head down, you just keep walking. A moment later and you reach the door that leads outside the fortress. You nearly run into Gordo, who's just on the way in.

"Turn around," you whisper, swooshing him back with your hands.

"Wha— oh," Gordo says as you grab his shoulders and turn him around in a neat little pirouette.

"Just keep walking," you say quietly. "I think I angered a bunch of blazes back there and we need to get out of there before they realize that I'm gone."

You check behind you, to see if they're following you.

They have *to be following me,* you think to yourself. But the room behind you is clear.

You start walking briskly, but not running along the ledge. You don't want to raise any alarm or concern.

You get almost to the end of the ledge and check back again. Still nothing. You've made it out safe! They're not following you.

Slowing down the pace, you take it easy as you approach the thin bridge you took to get here.

"We're good," you say to Gordo. "We can relax. Those dummies didn't even notice

I'd left…"

Gordo doesn't respond and you look up at him to see his reaction. This was supposed to be reassuring news, but Gordo is looking up at the sky, more worried than ever.

"No it's fine," you say.

"I don't know—" Gordo says.

"No, it *is*, I'm telling you. They didn't follow us so it's fine," you say a little impatiently.

"They didn't follow us… I don't know—" Your companion is still staring up worriedly.

"They didn't! Look," you turn pointedly to look back along the ledge you came form. "No blazes."

You feel Gordo's hands grasp the sides of your head and then he slowly tilts it up until you're looking at the sky.

There are seven swirling spots of gold and fire hovering in the air above you.

"Oh," you say in a trance, "So blazes can fly, eh?"

Then, a rain of fireballs comes down on your head.

THE END

To go back to the last choice and try again, *turn to page 56*. Or *flip to the beginning and choose a new story!*

"Hey don't worry about it," you tell Spark. "I'm sure it's all fine."

She doesn't seem totally convinced, but she drifts off into the centre of the room again. You glance back at her and then sneak over to the blaze that Spark called Flash.

She's spinning around and launching little tiny fireballs at the wall.

"Hey," you say cautiously. "How's it going?"

"Huh?" she stops spinning to look at you. "Oh, hi. I'm fine, I guess, trying to stay busy. What's up?"

"Oh, nothing," you say innocently.

She's suspicious. "But why are you talking to me?"

"Sorry," you say, "didn't mean to bother you. There was just something that Spark said, I thought you'd want to know…"

Flash glances over at Spark. "What?"

"She just said that you she was way better at flying than you…" you say. "She said Roast was better than you too. I mean, I guess you're the worst flyer in this whole room…"

"What?!" Flash fumes. "She didn't!"

"She did," you insist. "I don't know. Is it true?"

"Of course not!" Flash does a cool pirouette in the air. "I'm great at flying!"

You bite your lip. "Well, sorry then, I guess she just thinks some weird things. Excuse me, I've got to speak to Roast.

You slip away from the conversation, leaving Flash to glow brighter and angrier.

There's just a little more trouble to make…

"Hi, are you Roast?" you say to the blaze floating at the other edge of the room.

"Sure," he says. "Why?"

"Oh, I just wanted to ask you why you don't glow so bright?" you say innocently.

"What?!" he says with a sputtering of flame exploding from the centre of his smoky body. "What do you mean?"

"Oh, Spark and Flash were just saying that you're the worst glower, at least worse than them. I was just wondering why!"

"No!" Roast shouts. "That's not true! Oh, Spark's going to regret saying that!" The blaze shoots past you and towards Spark, floating far away .

That was easy, you think.

"DID YOU TELL THAT LITTLE GREEN THING THAT I DON'T GLOW BRIGHT!?" Roast screams at Spark, attracting the attention of the other blazes in the room.

"What, no?" Spark says, suddenly defensive.

Roast looks back at you with a glare, and you start to sweat.

"All I said," Spark continues, "was that Flash and I were probably the brightest glowers—"

"Oh no!" Roast cries. "I glow pretty dang bright, you're just so self-obsessed that you don't even notice it!"

"I'm not—" Spark sputters.

"YEAH!" Flash says, suddenly joining the conversation. "You're so self-obsessed that you think that you're better at flying than me!"

You look to your left and see that the commotion has attracted the other blazes into the room. Ember and the other three are standing nearby watching, concerned and confused.

"I didn't—" Spark says desperately. "What happened was that the green thing told me that Ember thought he was the best at flying and I just said that that's totally not true because Roast, or maybe me, are definitely the best flyer. Okay?"

"YOU SAID WHAT?!" Ember roars, shooting towards the other three blazes. "This is what I'm tired of! I'M CLEARLY THE BEST FLYER!"

"Oh heck no," says one of the blazes near you, following him. The other two jump after them, protesting and telling everyone to calm down.

But the other blazes don't take their advice. They only get more and more angry. Soon, they're all on fire and yelling. You can feel the heat on your face.

If you want to back up, *turn to page 124.*

If you want to stay where you are, *turn to page 111.*

What a wimp, you think. *That guy's scared of everything. This, right here, is time for greatness! It's time for bravery and seizing your destiny!*

You shake out of Gordo's grip and waddle as fast as you can towards the little hill that the players disappeared behind.

The heroes will get what they want and the fearful will be left in the dust, you think arrogantly as you race around the opposite side of the little bump in the ground.

Now where did they go? As you're about to come to the other side of the hill, you look off into the distance to see where the players have gone. But you don't see them on the horizon…

…because they're right in front of your face.

The two players are standing *right* behind the hill working on a little construction of obsidian.

You push back hard with your feet, trying to stop as quickly as possible so you don't run into them. You manage to stop a couple blocks away from the closest player.

You start backing up slowly. As long as you're quiet… you can make it out of here.

But then the other player looks up and sees you.

"ZOMBIE ALERT!" she howls and the white letters of her words appear in the sky above her head.

The other player jumps into action: his diamond pickaxe suddenly appears in his hand and he turns his square eyes on you. "I GOT IT," he thunders.

You turn and start running as fast as you can. But you don't make it far before you're clunked right in the back of the head with the heavy end of the pickaxe. Everything starts fading away and you know you're in trouble…

The last thing you hear before you poof out of existence is the female player remarking: "THAT'S FUNNY, I'VE NEVER SEEN A ZOMBIE RUN AWAY BEFORE…"

And then the diamond pickaxe comes down again.

Smack.

THE END

To go back to the last choice and try again, *turn to page 76. Or flip to the beginning and choose a new story!*

Scared of nothing, you stay exactly where you are as the blazes begin to hurl fireballs at each other.

They're all angry now, each one thinking that they're the best. They are like a pile of gunpowder. They only need a single spark to explode. And you were that spark.

You squint up at the glowing shapes flying through the air, and then all at once, they *explode*.

Fireballs fly everywhere, bathing the room. A bright red flame shoots right towards you. There's no time to move.

In a second, you're just a pile of roasted zombie.

There's no one there to witness, when a moment later, seven blaze rods clink to the floor quietly in an empty room.

THE END

To go back to the last choice and try again, *turn to page 106. Or flip to the beginning and choose a new story!*

"Honestly?" you say. "I'm trying to build a portal to the End, and I need some blaze rods to complete it. Do you guys think that I could have some? Can you spare about six?"

An angry crackling sound begins to fill the room. You look around in confusion.

"No, you guys don't understand," you try to explain. "You see, I *really* need it. It's a bit of a long story, but basically I need the rods so that I can get home—"

You are cut off by a whooshing sound as the blaze in front of you lights on fire. Their face is suddenly ringed by licking flames.

"Okay! Okay!" you say desperately, talking very fast. "I'll tell the story, I didn't know that you felt so strongly about— Okay, so it's a bit weird but I come from a different world and I play this game. This is *really* weird but the game is actually this world right here. Like, where I'm from—"

The rest of the blazes ignite with licking flames. Suddenly beads of sweat appear on your head. It's *very* hot.

You just keep talking faster. "—this whole world is just a game. Yeah, I know it's hard to get your brain around—"

"SILENCE!" the blaze in front of you roars.

You take a step backwards, bump into the blaze behind you, singe the back of your head and quickly step forward again.

"How can you be so ruuuuuude!" the blaze continues.

"Rude? I didn't mean to—" You're talking faster than you ever have before.

"You asked us for blaze rods!" another blaze roars. Even when the words are just crackles and pops, it's clear that the thing is angry.

"Yeah? I can do something in exchange—"

"BLAZE RODS ONLY COME FROM DEAD BLAZES!" the first blaze screams.

Your mouth hangs open dumbly.

"YOU HAVE ASKED US TO DIE! It is like if someone asked for corpses or skeletons! How incredibly ruuuuuude!"

Oh. You finally understand.

"WHAT DO YOU HAVE TO SAY FOR YOURSELF! ARE YOU NOT INCREDIBLY ASHAMED! WE SHOULD MAKE YOU PAY!" A fireball shoots out of the blaze and strikes the ceiling. The flames lick at the glowing stone.

The blazes seem very, very angry. You just made a mistake! You didn't know! You weren't trying to hurt anyone. But it doesn't look like they're about to let you off easy. Any second, one might fling their fireball right at you.

"WHAT DO YOU HAVE TO SAY FOR YOURSELF!"

If you say that you didn't know and tell them to take it easy, *turn to page 53.*

If you apologize profusely, *turn to page 56.*

There's a question nagging at your mind. You clear your throat and speak to the masses of pigmen. "How did your last chief become chief?" you ask.

There's a second of silence and then every pigman in the crowd tries to answer your question at once.

"SdofaoidguausdfasldladguadsfoasdfOINKsdouaiguuuudpants," the crowd says.

You wave your arms in the air. "Okay, okay, okay," you say. "That was my mistake. You!" You point at someone in the crowd. "How did your last chief become chief?"

The pigman steps forward a little shyly. "Well, the same way anyone becomes a chief," they say, as if it's obvious. "She beat up the last guy who was chief and everyone else was too scared to do anything about it…"

"Oh," you say.

"We're very glad that you're our new chief, oh powerful zombie!" the pigman says.

You nod. "Thanks, I can see why…" You make up your mind, and then say. "As your leader, there is one thing that I need to command you to do."

The pigmen nod excitedly. They can't wait to get bossed around!

"I command you to not make me your leader anymore!" you say.

The crowd erupts in confusion. There are a lot of alarmed oinks.

"I'll explain, I'll explain," you say. "I command, as *the zombie*, that your chief should not be the person who beat up the last chief, but the best person to lead your community. And they should be somebody that *everyone* chooses. Anyone who wants to be chief can come up here and make a speech about why they'd be the best chief, and then you'll all vote for the person you think is best. The one with the most votes becomes chief."

"Where does the beating come in?" one pigman asks.

"There's no beating!" you shout.

They seem to all think about that for a second. It's quite a strange idea for them.

The pigmen do as they're told and a couple line up at the edge of the platform, to give speeches. You step back and let them talk, and then when they're done, you ask the pigmen to vote by gathering around the candidate they like the best. You and Gordo count each group. One pigwoman, who said she wanted to make a lava pool in the middle of their island, received more than half the votes and you invite her up on the platform and put the black skull on top of her head.

"Your new chief!" you shout to the crowd, and they cheer, but you can tell they're a little weirded out about it. *They'll get used to it*, you think. The pigmen get to work planning a big party for their new chief and you decide it's time for you to sneak out of there. You grab Gordo's hand and lead him to the bridge through the chaos, but just as you're about to cross it, someone calls "Zombie!" from behind you.

You turn and see the new chief running up behind you.

"You've done something really good here," she says. "Our island is going to be much better without everyone beating each other up all the time. You can't leave now!"

"I have to," you say. "I'm on a quest—"

"Well, you have to take something as a gift, at least," she says and leads you to a little building of netherrack on the corner of the island. You go with her, just to be nice.

As she leads you through the door, you see inside and your breath is taken away. The whole room is full of beautiful, shiny odds and ends scattered all across the ground. There's a pile of emeralds, a couple diamonds, some wither skulls shoved in one corner, and best of all, some blaze rods scattered between your feet.

"This is where we keep the most valuable things that we find!" the pigwoman says with a smile. "You can have anything you want, perhaps one of these!" She holds up a feather. "It's very rare! Or how about these?!" She holds out some bones. "They're delicious."

You gather up an armful of blaze rods from the floor. "What about these?" you ask hopefully.

"Oh no," she says. "That's not enough. We find those around strongholds all the time. You're *the zombie*, you deserve the best!"

"No, this is good," you tell her. "I'll be okay." You thank her profusely and even though she begs you to take the feather, you excuse yourself and leave across the bridge with Gordo in tow.

Together, you weave your way back through the caverns. Only getting lost a couple times, you soon find yourself on the platform above the lava ocean. You help Gordo climb up the dangerous slope up to the cave where you started and wander back through the cave. The low, eerie purple light pulls you on, and soon you find yourself in front of the portal.

Together, you and Gordo step through the purple barrier and get yanked into the overworld. Luckily, it's night outside and you retrace your steps to Gordo's home village. Madame Mole is standing on her porch when you arrive and she calls out to you. She knows immediately, by the sound of your voice, that you have the blaze rods. The three of you descend into the stronghold below the village and wind your way to the room with the pool of lava and the end portal.

You grind the blaze rods into powder and sprinkle them over the ender pearls that you have. In a flash, the pearls grow a black spot in their centres: they are pupils. Creepily, the pearls start staring back at you. Except they are not pearls, they are eyes. Eyes of ender.

"Place them where they belong," Madame Mole says and you gather up the eyes in your arms and climb the stairs to the broken portal. You lean down and drop an eye into one of the gaping, open sockets in the stone frame. The stone closes around the eye. The eye spins around and stares directly at you. It watches you as you place the next eye, and then the next one and the next one.

The last eye locks into place and all the sound gets sucked out of the room. A thick black film spreads out between the twelve blocks that make up the portal. The eyes, for a moment, flash red.

And then they're back to staring at you.

You stare back, into the portal, into the blackness, into the path home. You lift one foot and start to jump…

THE END

Congratulations, you've reached one of the three happiest endings of this story. The story continues in The Zombie Adventure 4: Beginning of the End, *which is hitting shelves in 2018! There are two other endings in this book that lead to the next book in the series. Can you find them? To go back to the last choice and try again, turn to page 3, or turn to page 35 to go to the moment you entered the Nether and head off in a different direction, or flip to the beginning and choose a new story!*

Hi Reader,

Thanks so much for reading! I hope you really enjoyed this book!

If you've read this far in the series, you're a pretty big fan and I have to thank you so much for coming with me on this adventure. I'm sure you want me to keep writing more in this series and others, and **there's one way that you can help! Leaving a review** helps other people find the book which lets me keep writing. Please, I need your help, leave me a review on this book and everyone of mine that you've enjoyed!

It doesn't have to be a long review or well-written. Just search for *Zombie Adventure 3* on Amazon and click on this book. Scroll down and click on 'Write a Customer Review', click on the stars and write a couple words about what you thought of the book. It would mean so much to me! Thank you!

If you want to find out more about me and my books you can go to **johndiary.com**.

If you want to read more Choose Your Own Stories, you can get a free Choose Your Own Story book when you join my fan club at johndiary.com/signup. Just put in your e-mail address and I'll send you a book for free. Also I'll send you free previews of my books when they come out! And get the chance to win future books!

Flip to the back of the book to see sneak peeks of my other books!

You can also keep up with me online:

Facebook: John Diary at facebook.com/johndiarybooks

Twitter: @johndiarybooks

Instagram: johndiarybooks

Keep reading! Keep choosing!

You're the best,

John Diary

You say, "Alright! This way! We're almost there!"

They float along behind you as you weave further through the cavern. When you come to the portal, you look over your shoulder. The blazes are still following you, but some of them are moving slower. A couple of them have concerned looks on their faces.

"Don't worry, don't worry," you say. "We're almost there."

You shoo Gordo through the portal. "If it's not night out there," you whisper to him, "come back right away, okay?" He nods and then enters, but only after taking a couple big, panicked gulps of air.

Now it's just you, seven blazes and a purple, glowing portal. You wait a couplGordo doesn't come back through. The portal is still.

"Okay," you say with a cheery ring in your voice. "Now, this part is going to be a little weird, but you're going to have to trust me on this. I'm going to need you to come right up to me and float past me, to my right. You might feel a bit of a strange sensation. DO NOT FREAK OUT! DO NOT SHOOT FIREBALLS!"

You calm yourself down a bit. "This is just the first new, exciting thing that I'm going to show you."

The blazes seem pleased with this and the first one drifts towards you, past you and right into the purple portal. It sucks the blaze right in, and it disappears.

You call the next one up and it too slips through the portal. And then, one after the other, the five others follow suit.

Alone in the cavern, you cross your fingers and slip through the portal.

The invisible hook tugs at your belly button and the whole world disintegrates for a second, and then with a rude slap, it reassembles and a familiar landscape is all around you. You're back in the overworld. And a cool night is draped over the land.

You let yourself smile a little and look over at Gordo who is biting at his fingernails worriedly. "What are you DOING?" he mouths.

You ignore him.

"Okay everybody," you say to the blazes. "Here we go, open those eyes! You're in the overworld!"

The blazes do. They start spinning around wildly. Their eyes are bugging out of their heads. You watch one close their eyes again and then reopen them cautiously. They seem… agitated.

Uh oh.

"Is something wrong?" you ask. "Do you guys not like it? You can just close your eyes right away. I'll find another place." You're starting to panic.

The blazes say nothing.

"No," one says quietly. "I love it. I can't believe we're even here. In the overworld!"

The blazes start spreading out, leaning down to investigate the grass, drifting over to a tree to admire it. They stare at rocks and flowers and then a whole bunch of them are attracted to a nearby stream. They all just stare at that for ages.

You wander up behind them, a smile cracking at your lips.

"You like it?" you ask quietly.

"It's amazing," one says. "And best of all, it's dark!"

"Yeah," you say with a grin. "I thought you might like it here. Just one thing, before long, the sun is going to rise in the sky and you guys are going to *hate* that, so… try to find a cave or something before that happens okay."

No one really answers you, they're too distracted by the stream, but a couple of them nod and that seems good enough.

"Okay," you whisper. "I hope this makes things a little better. Again, I'm really sorry."

The blazes are still silent, absorbed in the babbling brook. You take that as your moment to slip off. You grab Gordo's hand and drag him away from the blazes and off into the night.

"What about the rods?" he says. "Did you get them?"

You shake your head. "Nah, there were more important things to do. Maybe we'll go and get them tomorrow."

"But—"

"It's okay," you assure him.

You walk a little longer and then you feel a tap only our shoulder.

"Gordo, knock it off," you say.

"Wasn't me," he says from your other side.

You turn around to see a blaze hovering softly above the ground beside you. There's something different about it… It's smiling.

"We love it here," the blaze says. "Thank you zombie. We're never going to leave. This is the place where we're meant to be."

For a second you wonder about what sort of chaos that is going to cause and then just shrug it off. You are just glad they're happy.

"You're so welcome, glad I could make it up to you," you say.

Something tumbles out of the blaze's spinning body. Several somethings. They are rods, and they're glowing bright.

You look up at the blaze with confusion. "I thought you said… But those are dead blazes!"

The blaze nods. "It's rude to ask for them. But when our friends and family die we keep all the rods, and we never have anything good to do with them anyways. You'll use them much better. Take them, it's only fair."

And with that, the blaze floats up and away.

You gather up the six blaze rods and head off through the night with Gordo at your side.

Madame Mole is standing on her porch when you arrive at Gordo's village and she calls out to you. She knows immediately, by the sound of your voice, that you have the blaze rods. The three of you descend into the fortress below the village and wind your way to the room with the pool of lava and the end portal.

You grind the blaze rods into powder and sprinkle them over the ender pearls that you have. In a flash, the pearls grow a black spot in their centres: they are pupils. Creepily, the pearls start staring back at you. Except they are not pearls, they are eyes. Eyes of ender.

"Place them where they belong," Madame Mole says and you gather up the eyes in your arms and climb the stairs to the broken portal. You lean down and drop an eye into one of the gaping, open sockets in the stone frame. The stone closes around the eye. The eye spins around and stares directly at you. It watches you as you place the next eye, and then the next one and the next one.

The last eye locks into place and all the sound gets sucked out of the room. A think black film spreads out between the twelve blocks that make up the portal, the eyes, for a moment, flash red.

And then they're back to staring at you.

You stare back, into the portal, into the blackness, into the path home. You lift one foot and start to jump…

THE END

Congratulations, you've reached one of the three happiest endings of this story. The story continues in The Zombie Adventure 4: Beginning of the End, *which is hitting shelves in 2018! There are two other endings in this book that lead to the next book in the series. Can you find them? To go back to the last choice and try again, turn to page 60, or turn to page 35 to go to the moment you entered the Nether and head off in a different direction, or flip to the beginning and choose a new story!*

Hi Reader,

Thanks so much for reading! I hope you really enjoyed this book!

If you've read this far in the series, you're a pretty big fan and I have to thank you so much for coming with me on this adventure. I'm sure you want me to keep writing more in this series and others, and **there's one way that you can help! Leaving a review** helps other people find the book which lets me keep writing. Please, I need your help, leave me a review on this book and everyone of mine that you've enjoyed!

It doesn't have to be a long review or well-written. Just search for *Zombie Adventure 3* on Amazon and click on this book. Scroll down and click on 'Write a Customer Review', click on the stars and write a couple words about what you thought of the book. It would mean so much to me! Thank you!

If you want to find out more about me and my books you can go to **johndiary.com**.

If you want to read more Choose Your Own Stories, you can get a free Choose Your Own Story book when you join my fan club at johndiary.com/signup. Just put in your e-mail address and I'll send you a book for free. Also I'll send you free previews of my books when they come out! And get the chance to win future books!

Flip to the back of the book to see sneak peeks of my other books!

You can also keep up with me online:

Facebook: John Diary at facebook.com/johndiarybooks

Twitter: @johndiarybooks

Instagram: johndiarybooks

Keep reading! Keep choosing!

You're the best,

John Diary

You take a couple steps back just in time. A second later the fireballs start to fly. They scorch the stone you were standing on.

All the blazes are hurling insults and balls of fire at each other. Each one thinks they're the best at everything.

Blazes are kind of hotheads, you think, and then giggle to yourself.

Suddenly you realize that you can't even see the blazes anymore. They are all just one big giant ball of fire. It explodes out towards you and you cover your face to protect yourself from the heat.

You cough at the smoke. When you look up again, the air is empty. There are no blazes.

Running over to the edge of the balcony, you look down and see several glowing rods on the floor of the bigger chamber.

With a grin you run down to pick up the rods and race back out to meet Gordo. He's standing outside the entrance to the fortress with a worried look on his face.

"Oh Rotney!" he says with relief, "you're still alive!"

You nod. "Better than alive," you say, showing him the rods in your arms.

A smile slides across his face.

"You don't smile much," you say to him as you walk along the ledge and over the bridge.

"Nothing makes me happier than being able to go home..." he says, and you laugh.

Together, you weave your way back through the cave you spawned in. The low, eerie purple light pulls you on, and soon your find yourself in front of the portal.

You and Gordo step through the purple barrier and get yanked into the overworld. Luckily, it's night outside and you retrace your steps to Gordo's home village. Madame Mole is standing on her porch when you arrive and she calls out to you. She knows immediately, by the sound of your voice, that you have the blaze rods.

The three of you descend into the stronghold below the village and wind your way to the room with the pool of lava and the end portal.

You grind the blaze rods into powder and sprinkle them over the ender pearls that you have. In a flash, the pearls grow a black spot in their centres: they are pupils. Creepily, the pearls start staring back at you. Except they're not pearls, they're eyes. Eyes of ender.

"Place them where they belong," Madame Mole says and you gather up the eyes in your arms and climb the stairs to the broken portal. You lean down and drop an eye into one of the gaping, open sockets in the stone frame. The stone closes around the eye. The eye spins around and stares directly at you. It watches you as you place the next eye, and then the next one and the next one.

The last eye locks into place and all the sound gets sucked out of the room. A think black film spreads out between the twelve blocks that make up the portal. The eyes, for a moment, flash red.

And then they're back to staring at you.

You stare back, into the portal, into the blackness, into the path home. You lift one foot and start to jump…

THE END

Congratulations, you've reached one of the three happiest endings of this story. The story continues in The Zombie Adventure 4: Beginning of the End, *which is hitting shelves in 2018! There are two other endings in this book that lead to the next book in the series. Can you find them? To go back to the last choice and try again, turn to page 106, or turn to page 35 to go to the moment you entered the Nether and head off in a different direction, or flip to the beginning and choose a new story!*

Hi Reader,

Thanks so much for reading! I hope you really enjoyed this book!

If you've read this far in the series, you're a pretty big fan and I have to thank you so much for coming with me on this adventure. I'm sure you want me to keep writing more in this series and others, and **there's one way that you can help! Leaving a review** helps other people find the book which lets me keep writing. Please, I need your help, leave me a review on this book and everyone of mine that you've enjoyed!

It doesn't have to be a long review or well-written. Just search for *Zombie Adventure 3* on Amazon and click on this book. Scroll down and click on 'Write a Customer Review', click on the stars and write a couple words about what you thought of the book. It would mean so much to me! Thank you!

If you want to find out more about me and my books you can go to **johndiary.com.**

If you want to read more Choose Your Own Stories, you can get a free Choose Your Own Story book when you join my fan club at johndiary.com/signup. Just put in your e-mail address and I'll send you a book for free. Also I'll send you free previews of my books when they come out! And get the chance to win future books!

Sneak peaks of my other books are on the next couple pages!

You can also keep up with me online:

Facebook: John Diary at facebook.com/johndiarybooks

Twitter: @johndiarybooks

Instagram: johndiarybooks

Keep reading! Keep choosing!

You're the best,

John Diary

If you liked this book, you'll love the heart-warming and gut-busting tale of Sneezy Steve. He has just spawned in the world of Minecraft with nothing: no memories, no items and no clue what to do next. The only thing he *does* have is a mysterious photograph of a girl with orange hair in the bottom of his backpack.

What happens next? I can't even say, because it's all up to you. Will Steve ask a sheep for directions? Will he become best friends with an old block of dirt? Maybe you'll help him look for the girl in the photograph. Or maybe you'll not be so helpful and turn him into a zombie, or make him pretend to be a wolf. The choice is yours in my brand new series!

Dan is playing Minecraft with his friends, like he always does, when a strange figure, white from head-to-toe, approaches him in the game and drops a book at his feet. Cautiously, Dan reads the book: it's an invitation, to a school. A school for only the very best Minecraft players in the country.

It all seems to good to be true.

And maybe it is…

In the second Sneezy Steve book, Steve is faced with a mystery, all the Creepers in the whole world all seem to be on the march. In the hundreds and thousands, they are all walking... somewhere.

Take control of Steve and his world and weave your own story through this holiday adventure. Will you save Christmas? Or join the dastardly plot to make the biggest bomb in Minecraft history? Will your best friend Alex go with you on your journey? And if not, how are you going to keep Steve from getting in trouble while surrounded by literally every creeper in the world. This... is going to be a tough one.

Made in the USA
Monee, IL
20 September 2021